PRESSING HARD

C.H

PRESSING HARD

STEPHANIE PERRY MOORE

KENSINGTON PUBLISHING CORP.
http://www.kensingtonbooks.com

DAFINA BOOKS are published by

Kensington Publishing Corp.
850 Third Avenue
New York, NY 10022

All Kensington titles, imprints and distributed lines are available at special quantity discounts for bulk purchases for sales promotion, premiums, fund-raising, educational or institutional use.

Special book excerpts or customized printings can also be created to fit specific needs. For details, write or phone the office of the Kensington Special Sales Manager: Kensington Publishing Corp., 850 Third Avenue, New York, NY 10022. Attn. Special Sales Department. Phone: 1-800-221-2647.

Dafina Books and the Dafina logo Reg. U.S. Pat. & TM Off.

ISBN-13: 978-0-7582-1872-8
ISBN-10: 0-7582-1872-9

First Kensington Trade Paperback Printing: September 2007
10 9 8 7 6 5 4 3 2

Printed in the United States of America

For Tony Brown

(My senior class prom date)

Ahhh . . . stories to tell, and I pray that
you and yours are well.
The pressure was on!
May these young people push His way.

Acknowledgments

When I first wrote the Payton Skky series, I had no pressure. Shucks, the first two books weren't even picked up. Nine years later, it's a different ballgame. I prayed for an increase in my writing life and now the pressure is most certainly on. I have deadlines big time, and my publisher needs the work on time. Some days I feel like doing nothing. Thankfully, through prayer, God gives me the strength to push through my laziness and get done what He has blessed me to be able to do.

When writing a book on peer pressure, I'm clearly aware that life as a teen hasn't gotten easier. One person is probably trying to get you to try this and others want you to do that. However, I hope this book helps you to understand that you have the power to stay right where God wants you. Apply positive pressure back to your friends and be the leader He has called you to be. Tugging people toward greatness is an awesome thing. And here's a shout out to everyone who moves my dream along.

To my family, parents Dr. Franklin and Shirley Perry, Sr., brother, Dennis, and sister-in-law, Leslie, my mother-in-law, Ms. Ann, and extended family, Bobby and Sarah Lundy, what a blessing you are. I'm thankful for your support. It's hard being on this writing journey, but you always push me through.

To my publisher, Dafina Books, and especially my editor, Selena James, I'm excited about your passion for this series. The edge you give the manuscript takes it to the limit. Thanks for really making this project become something we pray will change the lives of a generation.

For my writing team, Jason Spelling, Carolyn Ohora, Calvin Johnson, James Johnson, Ciara Roundtree, Jessica Phillips, Randy Roberts, Ron Whitehurst, Vanessa Davis Griggs, Larry Spurill, John Rainey and Teri Anton, you forced me to not stop writing till it was right. I'm blessed that you cared enough to take time and give wisdom. The hard-core themes in this book will reach even more readers because you didn't let up the pressure.

To the special young men in my life, Leon Thomas, Franklin Perry III, Kadarius Moore, Dakari Jones, Dorian Lee, and Danton Lynn, I love you. I hope this novel can be a guide to help you stay on course. Grow to be men who follow the Lord.

To my girlfriends' sons, Devan Dixon, Colby Clark, Breshad Perriman, Antonio Jr. and Austin London, Bryant Bolds II, Roy Palmer Jr., Brandon and Brian Bradley, Justin and Jordan Peace, and Chandler, Canyon, and Cole Smith, the words within these pages were written with you in mind. I'm praying, with your moms, for your lives to please God. Work hard to make Him proud.

To my spunky chicks, Sydni and Sheldyn, thanks for making me smile. One day you'll like the fellas. I'm praying this title serves as a resource to show you what type of guy God has for you.

To my new world of readers, thanks for allowing this series a place in your busy world. Move to stand for Him. Believe that you can be cool and still do things God's way.

And to my Almighty Father, thanks for breathing truth into this book. I'm thrilled to be writing from the male perspective. May every reader press hard to please You above all things.

Contents

Contents

~ 1 ~

Grooving too Much

"You a punk. A little mama's boy. That's why you won't have a drink," Damarius taunted as I helped him carry beer from the car to his house for the New Year's Eve jam he was about to host.

I was tired of it. He could call me whatever he wanted to. Say whatever he wanted to say. I didn't care. He wasn't going to pressure me into doing something I wasn't ready to do.

"Come on, Cole," Damarius said, looking to our friend for back up. "You need to admit it too. That's what you think of his tail. Do you think he all that? He hadn't never even had a piece, drank a little nip or smoked a joint. Dang! Perry ain't no real man yet."

I wanted to take one of those six packs and bust him across the head with it. But because we were late setting things up, I let it go. As we entered the house, Cole spoke up.

"All right you two. Kiss and make up," he said before Damarius and I went our separate ways.

It didn't take the place long to fill up. Not only were there a lot of kids from my school in the house, but folks from all over Augusta were showing up. I felt sort of bad that I didn't call my girl, Savoy, but honestly the whole commitment thing was scaring me a bit. I didn't want to feel pressured into a relationship with her. I hadn't seen her since Christmas night, but I thought about her all the time.

As I walked around scanning the crowd, I thought about Damarius accusing me of being a punk. So if a brother didn't get high or get wasted, then he wasn't cool? I knew Damarius was just jealous. I didn't need anything to make me feel good about me. I was high off of life. College coaches were always trying to persuade me to change my choice from going to Georgia Tech. Girls always trying to get with me. Brothers always wanting me to attend their functions or just to hang out with them to raise their stock with the ladies. I had it like that.

At that moment, none of that meant a thing to me. I wanted respect from my boy. Was proving to him that I could handle alcohol the only way I could get him off my back? I don't know why I was letting him get to me. Maybe I should just pray about it. After all, I had learned this year that if I just give it to God, He'd make my situation better.

Deep down I had to admit that I felt as if I was at the sidelines looking on. I peered in like I was watching this stuff on the TV or something. Maybe I had issues and I needed to release, let go, and get down.

When I stepped into the hallway, I saw Jaboe, a thug from down the block. Jaboe was a high school dropout who should have graduated with my sister's class two years ago, but he started selling drugs. He told the world that he could make way more money hustling than he ever could the legitimate way.

"Hey man. I'm good for it! You ain't gotta jack me up like that," Damarius told Jaboe as the thug grabbed him by his collar and squeezed it tight.

What did my boy get himself into? It was hard for me to believe that he was doing drugs. The pressure of wanting to get into a major college had given my buddy a new perspective on right and wrong.

"I want some bills, boy. I don't want no change," Jaboe said as he slung the coins in his hand to the floor. "You got all these folks in here for free. You better start charging some money next time you have a party 'cause I want my paper. If I don't get it next week, not only will you be cut off from the stash," he said as he took a knife out of his pocket and put it to Damarius's face, "but you know what else is next."

Damarius tried talking his way of out the problem. "All right, dude. Ease up! I'm gonna get yo' money. Give me a little credit. You know I'm good for it."

I had no idea that my boy was smoking more than cigarettes. No wonder his grades were slipping.

Regardless of how he felt about me, I had to stop him from messing his life up. Like Reverend McClep preached at church last Sunday, I was my brother's keeper. I wasn't going to let Damarius go down like that. I saw Jaboe pull out a dime bag and I quickly intercepted it, as if I was a defensive back on the field or something and tossed it back up in his face. "He doesn't want that," I said to Jaboe.

I looked over his shoulder at the two guys with him. One had cornrows with even parts going down to the back of his head and a grill, and the other dude was thicker than Mr. T himself. They stepped toward me, but I wasn't backing down. I didn't care how long Damarius had been messing around with that stuff. It was going to end today.

"Come on, Perry. What's up? You crazy? This is business," Damarius said to me.

"Is there a problem?" Jaboe asked, his eyes threatening.

"No, man, there ain't no problem," Damarius said, stepping between us.

"Like D said, no problem. He just don't need your stuff. So thanks for coming," I said, pointing to the front door.

"What's up, Damarius? You gonna let him talk for you? Or a betta question, you gonna let him talk to me like that?" Jaboe pulled up his sweater and showed us he was packing.

Throwing my hands up, I said, "I don't mean no disrespect Jaboe. Look, he just don't need it, all right?"

"Yeah, I hear you." He laughed and dropped his top, concealing the weapon again. "Cool, I ain't trying to push my stuff off on anybody, but I do want my money."

"You'll get it. Soon, man," Damarius promised.

Jaboe and his gangster boys left. Damarius tried to go off on me about the whole thing.

Getting in my face, he said, "Man! What's up? Are you crazy? You'll mess up your whole life getting in Jaboe's way."

I couldn't believe he tried to play me instead of thank me. "You need to pay him the little money you owe him and leave him alone before you end up like him, on the corner somewhere. He's reduced to hiding out from the cops and bullying folks into giving him dollars."

"You don't know what you just did, Perry. Stay out of my business," he said, shaking his head as he walked past me to join the crowd in the livingroom. I was just about to leave the party when I heard Damarius announce over the DJ's system, "Hey y'all! Hey y'all! Y'all know my boy Perry here don't drink, right?"

What he was doing? Why was he calling me out like that?

"But it's New Year's Eve, and we want him to have a little fun, right y'all?" The crowd started chanting, "Yeaaa, Perry! Drink! Drink! Drink!"

I went over to him and whispered, "What's up with this?"

"You all up in my business! You can't knock what I enjoy until you try it. Was I right earlier, Perry? Are you a punk?"

Without even thinking, I took the beer out of his hand, twisted off the top, and gulped it down. I didn't even have time to decide if I liked the taste or not. A random guy from the crowd ran up to me with another one. I wasn't no punk. Damarius was not about to play me like that. I twisted off the cap and chugged that one down, too.

"Drink! Drink! Drink! Drink!" folks called out.

"Can you handle one more, big boy?" Damarius dared.

Cole came up said, "Man, that's enough. What you trying to do to him, D?"

"I can handle it. I'll show you it ain't all that. Give me another one." All I could hear was more chanting from the crowd when I drank the next brew.

After a few minutes I was feeling a little light-headed. But it was all good. Someone handed me another one with the top already off. I couldn't tell if someone had drunk out of it or not, but it really didn't matter. I drank it down, and when I was done, the crowd yelled and screamed louder than fans did at any football game I'd ever played in. I was feeding off of it. A couple of girls came up to me and got close: one in the front and one in the back. They swayed their hips from left and to right, and my hips started moving too. Oh, the party was on.

Damarius came up to me. "Dang, man. You can hold your stuff. All right. All right. My bad." He laughed and walked away.

After a couple of dances, I went up to the DJ and started trying to spin records, which I have no skills with at all on a regular day. But being a little intoxicated, nobody could tell me that I wasn't the life of the party. The sad thing was that I couldn't go anywhere without the two girls, Q and Jo, following me. It was cute, but I was getting tired of them.

"You know what? Y'all gotta give a brother some space. Dang, I can't even dance with nobody else."

They looked as if I had hurt their feelings.

"I'm sorry. I'm just being honest."

"You all right, boy?" Damarius said as he came over to me and handed me another beer. "I thought you wanted this. I didn't want you to have to look for it."

Cole grabbed it out of my hand. "No, no, D. He done had enough for real."

"Whatcha mean, I done had enough?"

"Tell 'em. Perry, tell 'em. You feeling good right about now, right?" Damarius said.

"Good? I feel the same. Whatcha talking about?"

I was so out of it, I didn't even know what Damarius was talking about.

"Naw, Perry." Cole said, turning away.

"Man, give me that beer!" I grabbed the beer out of my boy's hand, spilling some of it on the floor. Sipping the beer, I stepped around my boys so I could get back to dancing.

I stopped and had to blink my eyes a couple of times when I saw my ex, Tori, standing in the middle of a crowd. She still looked as fine as she always did. Her hair was all done up, her nails were manicured just right, and she was wearing this cute little pink number that hugged her body just right.

"What's up girl? Dang. A brother can't get no love."

She yanked my hand and pulled me down the hall. She pushed me into Damarius's bedroom and shut the door.

"Uhh-ha. What's up? You wanna give yourself to me now? I just asked for a hug. I didn't know you wanted to give it up."

"Perry, I love you too much to see you act like this. What's going on?"

"What you talking about? Dang! You pulled me up in here. I don't need no girl giving me a hard time by telling me what to do. We don't go together no more, and I guess I should be glad of that."

"You making a fool of yourself tonight, okay."

"Man, I'm the life of this joint."

"No, people are staring at you because you are tripping over yourself. Drool is coming out of your mouth. It's clear you can't hold alcohol."

"Girl, shut up. Leave me alone. Bye. Get out. I'm sorry I asked for some love. I got another girl. She's prettier than you."

The moment I said that, I wanted to take my words back, but I knew that wasn't possible because Tori had heard me. She looked devastated. I felt bad. I didn't mean to hurt her, but the alcohol was speaking.

"You got somebody else?"

"Forget it. Forget it. I just need to be alone."

"I mean, you just said it! You said you got somebody else! Talk to me! Tell me! Is it somebody at our school? Is it somebody I know? We haven't been broke up but a couple of months, and you already got another girlfriend?"

"I ain't said I had another girlfriend. Dang. Y'all females be tripping."

"I'm not tripping. I should have expected it. I mean, everywhere I go, girls are telling me I'm stupid for letting you go and not giving it up. If they not telling me that, they telling me they plan to satisfy you. So hey, I'm not surprised. I might as well have a drink with you," she said as she came over, trying to get what was left in my bottle.

"Go on now. You don't need this. Seriously. Look, look!" I said as I shoved her to the side.

I didn't mean to push her, but again, I didn't have complete control of my faculties. What was supposed to be just a little push moved her halfway across the room towards the door.

"Okay. Fine. I get it. You don't have to hurt me worse than you already have, okay." She opened the door and dashed out.

After she left, I stood staring at the open door, upset and confused. I realized what I had done, and I wanted to go after her, but I began to feel a terrible burning sensation in my chest. What was going on?

I couldn't understand why I was having such horrible physical pain. It was like I was having a heart attack or something. I couldn't even make it to Damarius's bed. I fell straight to the floor. I couldn't breathe. I felt like I was going to die.

The only thing I could do was pray: *Lord, I'm sorry. You gotta help me, though. I was stupid to drink. Being pressured and all. Yeah, I gotta admit it felt good for a minute, but right now, I feel worse than as if three linebackers tackled me. Please Lord, please.*

I couldn't even pray anymore. I looked up at Damarius's light, which was circling around and around in his room, thinking about all the hopes and dreams I had for myself. I wondered if this was going to be the end. Stupidity might have done me in. Maybe Tori was right about me thinking I was cool. I had not only hurt her feelings, but also I'd probably made a complete idiot out of myself. All of a sudden, I heard the door open. I didn't know who it was, but I certainly didn't want anyone to see me unable to keep my composure. But there was nothing I could do about that now.

"Perry, man, what's up? What's up?" Cole yelled as he rushed to my side.

"I don't feel good, man." I was so happy to see him.

"See. I told Damarius you didn't need all that beer."

"Man, what am I suppose to do? My chest is burning for real."

"You gotta take deep breaths."

"You ever felt like this?"

"I gotta get you some water."

"Water? That's gonna help?"

"I'll be right back. Just hold on."

My boy left and it seemed like it was taking him forever to come back. *Why did teenagers drink?* I started asking myself. At first I could feel it. There was some pleasure in it. It made me feel good, confident, and larger than life. Now here I was, helpless. When I heard the door open again, I yelled, "Call the ambulance."

"See, I told you he was hurting," Cole said to Damarius.

"He'll be all right. Just give him the doggone water. Boy, you can't hold nothing."

I drank the water and took deep breaths as they helped me onto Damarius's bed.

"You just need to rest and relax."

"I still don't feel good y'all, for real."

"Dang! I gotta bring the party in here. Nobody gonna believe this. He can't hold his own."

I didn't even care at that moment. But I heard Cole taking up for me.

I lay in that bed for the next five minutes, vowing to the Lord that I would never ever go over the top with alcohol again if I survived this situation. I thought about my parents, and how this would let them down. They had raised me better than that, even though all my life I had been pushed by my peers to do stuff. I'd always been the leader, applying positive peer pressure. But here I was caught up in the wrong mess. I was trying to keep Damarius from smoking his brains away, and he turns around and pushes me to put something I don't need into my body. I now knew none of this was worth it. Trying to impress people. Trying to be in the in-crowd. All that stuff was silly. I had to stay in my lane and run my race. As I took a deep breath and watched my chest rise higher and higher, I hated that I was grooving too much.

~ 2 ~

Managing the Damage

Oh man! The smooth touch going up and down my leg felt so good. The tickling on my chest made me laugh. Kisses and hugs encompassed me as I was immersed in every man's dream. Well, not every man, but at least all my boys would have died to be in my place in this fantasy. Two chicks were kissing me from top to bottom. I couldn't do nothing but enjoy every moment. I realized I was feeling better than I had hours before, when all that beer had gotten to me. I was startled by a voice beside me.

"Don't get up now. We were just beginning to have fun."

It was one of the girls from earlier and she bit my neck real hard.

"Ouch!" I said.

Unable to say more, as my attention was diverted to the female on the other side. Here I was, about to thank God for this extra time on the earth and I looked down at my bare chest, peeked under the covers, and saw that I had nothing on. What in the world had I gotten myself into? What had I done with these doggone girls? I jumped out of the bed fast, pulling the covers around me. That's when I noticed they needed the covers too.

"This is crazy. Did we—did we do something?" I questioned.

I didn't remember going that far in my dream. Quickly, I scanned the room for my clothes, but I couldn't find them anywhere.

"Y'all seen my stuff?"

"We're just glad you're okay," the one I called Q said.

"How'd y'all know I was in here? I mean, I do remember being passed out. What's up?"

Jo got out of the bed like a tiger, came up to me, and scratched my chest.

"You like it rough, don't you?"

"Ahh, no. Put on some clothes. Please."

I had to get a handle on this. This just wasn't me. This wasn't right. Not only did I not remember what had gone on between us, but now fully comprehending what could have gone down, I knew I wouldn't have signed off on that. I had been keeping my distance from Savoy, trying not to let my feelings for her grow too deep. But now I knew I was gonna have to make sure I stayed away from her so she wouldn't fall out with me. There was no way I could explain that, and now I was all scratched up with evidence on my neck.

"What's wrong? We're not making you feel good enough?" Q said.

I had to get out of there.

I searched the room until I found my clothes in a neat pile under the bed. I dressed, then walked right out into the crowd as they counted down, *Three, two, one.* Instead of cheering for Happy New Year, they cheered my name. This was all the way messed up. Tori was the first person that I came eye to eye with, and she looked devastated as Jo and Q walked up behind me. I grabbed Jo by the arm and took her down the hall.

"Look, this isn't a game to me. Tell me straight up what happened in there."

"Nothing boy. You were asleep. You talked in your sleep and snored a little bit. Before we could get the party started, you ran out. Satisfied?"

Oh, I felt so good hearing that. I left Jo standing there and went to the bathroom to splash cold water on my face.

Lord, I'm not making it easy for You to do your job. I'm sorry.

"Man, let me in. Let me in," Damarius said as he banged on the door. I was ready to take on any of his bull. He didn't let me down when he sucked his teeth and said, "Them girls in there told me you wasn't about nothing. Sent two in there for you, and you still couldn't enjoy yourself. Dang, boy. Even drunk you too straight up."

"And I guess that's the way I like it. You might better be glad too or I might have needed to borrow some of your pills. You know, to clear up anything I could have contracted from them."

"Oh see. Now you ain't got to go there."

"No, I'm just trying to be straight up."

I opened the door and headed for the front of the house. Damarius followed me. I didn't care that he was trying to front on me. Nothing he could say was going to rock my boat again. I'd been there and done that. I was back in the driver's seat of my own life, and I wasn't down for having no more wrecks.

When I pulled up at my house at 2:15 AM, all the lights were on. I knew that wasn't a good sign, but I figured if I just told my dad about the night's events he'd be straight with everything. After all, I'd be graduating in a few months. Certainly he would be cool with me having a little fun. But when I got in the door, before I could speak he grabbed my collar and yelled, "Negro, your mama and I been worried about you. You know this is the night that all those drunks are out there riding the streets. You could have called someone if you knew you were going to be late. This is just what I'm talking about being responsible. Missing your curfew. If you would have missed curfew with your coach you'd be in some serious trouble, and maybe your butt would be kicked off the team. You really think you ready to go to college?"

Every time I tried to open my mouth, he kept going. My trying to say anything on my behalf was not possible. It's like he wanted to stay mad at me. Why the heck did we have to start the year off like this when we'd just ended the previous year by getting our father-son relationship back on track?

"I was just trying to tell you." I paused when he sniffed my mouth.

"Ahh, heck naw, boy. You been drinking."

"What? What?" my mom said all frantic. "Perry, come on, you're kidding me, baby. I know you haven't been drinking."

"This boy done had some beers and not just one. I've got to ground your tail again. You're gonna wind up dead or killing somebody else and ruining your whole career before it ever really takes off. Son, I ain't trying to be tough on you for me. This is for your own good."

"Could you just take your hands off me, Pops? Dang. I'm trying to explain."

"There ain't nothing you can say to me about why you been drinking beer, why you tail came into the house late tonight, and why you drove home all inebriated."

"Son, just go on up and go to bed," my mom said.

"Naw, see that's the problem. He can't be a man if you don't let me discipline his tail. Just because he's in the twelfth grade he thinks I can't tell him nothing."

"I'm not saying that, honey. You two can't accomplish anything all upset and angry."

"Dad," I said before I walked away, "believe it or not, I let my boys punk me, all right. I had a little too much to drink, and you don't know how much I regret it. I wasn't thinking clearly, but I didn't get into the car until I knew I could walk a straight line."

I knew that was a lie and looking at my dad's face, he wasn't buying it.

"Okay, okay, so maybe I was wrong not to call y'all, but again, I wasn't thinking straight. I am sorry though. Punish me or do whatever. Whatever you do won't be worse than the lesson I learned for myself. My chest was burning, Dad. I mean, I'm sorry." I headed to my room not knowing whether my parents were cool with what I said. They were right, I did owe them an explanation and once I gave it, I felt cool to fall out on my bed, shoes and all. I was hoping they wouldn't continue to hold this against me.

The next morning I awoke to breakfast in bed. My mom had those pancakes, eggs and sausages smelling up something. The maple syrup was heated up and a tall glass of orange juice was calling my name.

"Thanks Mom." I grabbed my mom's hand. "I'm sorry about last night, for real."

"Perry, your father and I talked some this morning, sweetie. What you said made a lot of sense. You had a little too much to drink, giving in to peer pressure, and you got sick. That's a good lesson. I'm just thankful you got home in one piece and that you woke up this morning. Looks like you're in your right mind. I see the way you're eyeing my pancakes."

"I love you, Mom," I chuckled.

I didn't even realize I had my fork and knife in hand ready to cut into them.

"Dad here?"

"Yeah. He said he'll come in here in a little while."

"He's still upset with me?"

"I don't think he's so upset as much as he is disappointed. He cares about you, baby, and although he's got a tough way of communicating with you, he does all that he does because he wants you to be the best young man you can be. Morally, athletically, and definitely spiritually. Eat up, eat up."

It took me all of five minutes to devour all that she had prepared. My dad came in after I ate my last bite.

"So you felt sick last night, huh?"

"Dad, I swear my chest was burning."

"We need to talk about that. That's how young men die like that in college. Payton told me about an incident last fall that happened at the University of Georgia. You start letting guys punk you like that then they will slip drugs into your drink. Your body can't handle it. Your butt will be in the hospital. You know?"

"Yeah. I hear you, Dad. I hear you."

"I just want you to be the bigger man. Nobody's ever talked you into doing anything you didn't want to do. I've seen you around your friends. They'll make an argument to do something stupid, but before they know what hit them you've talked them into taking the higher ground, and you stay so cool. I just don't understand what happened last night." My dad left, closing the bedroom door behind him.

I couldn't tell my dad Damarius tried to buy some weed. He might cut me off from hanging out with my boy, and that to me wasn't the right way to go about solving anything. I mean, even Jesus went to win the whoremongers and drunkards. I know I'm not Jesus, but I did feel a sense of urgency to try to help my boy. He knows he doesn't need to get high to be happy. Later today, I was going to tell him that fact, and if we end up not friends anymore, then so be it.

My phone rang. No name came up, so I didn't answer it. I went about pulling out the clothes I was going to put on.

The big BCS games would be coming on later that day, and I was ready to hang out with my pops and watch some football. Then my phone rang again. It was some crazy number. I picked it up.

"What's up? Who is this?"

"You need to take a look at your e-mail."

"Who is this?" I said, not recognizing the crazy, weird voice.

"Take a look at your e-mail. I'll hit you back."

I went over to my computer. I was ticked. I couldn't get on it. I had to get the virus off of it. Finally, though, I was able to sign on. There was an e-mail message with a video message attachment. As soon as I clicked on it, I almost threw up my mom's delicious meal when I saw myself lying in bed beside a bag of weed, a couple of beer bottles, and two girls who were rubbing all over me.

"What the heck is this?" One girl was on top of me and another talking. Then there was a male voice, off-camera, imitating my voice, giving directions to the girls on where to touch me. It continued.

"You want another hit?" one of the girls asked. Then I saw a little white, rolled up shriveled object get placed in my mouth. It looked like my eyes were closed, but it was hard to tell. I pushed back the chair, stood, and began pacing. If this tape got released to the news—local news, CNN, Fox, or ESPN, I would be completely messed up. There were only a few weeks before national signing day. This video could ruin all of that. All of a sudden, the tape went to Jaboe's face.

"So look here bro'. You need to keep your nose out of my affairs. Half the kids up in this party are my clients, like your boy Damarius. He owes me a wad of cash, and I intend to collect it. You get in the way, and I'm gonna mess you up. You leave my game alone, and I won't mess up your play. Understand? I'm in control."

The screen went to black. This was crazy. I wanted to save

Damarius from himself, but right about now I clearly got the message. I first had to worry about me. My phone rang. Looking at the same crazy number, I answered the phone.

"Why are you doing this to me?" I asked.

"Oh, like you don't know, partner. I said it all on the tape. Do we have an understanding? Am I in control or what?"

I paused and said in a low tone, "You in control."

"I didn't hear you!" Jaboe shouted through the receiver.

"You're in control." I said, more firmly.

"Great. Can I look forward to cheering you on next year in the stands? You plan to watch some of the games today, man?"

He went on talking to me like we were boys or something.

"I got your message."

"All right. All right that's cool. I'm out." He hung up.

After I hung up the phone, I quickly shut down my computer. I wished there was a way I could go in and erase the video, even off of Jaboe's computer. I felt so humiliated. But I had to be real. I had to do what I had to do to keep Perry Skky Jr. clean in the press. Although I didn't feel great, I felt good about managing the damage.

~ 3 ~

Getting It Straight

Dang! *I hate I can't get Savoy out of my mind*, I thought to myself as I flipped the switch for the gas fireplace in my home and sat down in front of it.

The month of January was practically over. I hadn't talked to Savoy since Christmas. Granted, we had e-mailed each other and left each other messages. I'd even gotten a cute little card in the mail from her. It was lavender-scented. I really didn't know what was up with me, and why I wasn't pursuing her. I kept thinking about her, but I wasn't doing anything about my feelings.

I guess since Tori got a little too manic on me, maybe on a subconscious level I was trying to avoid all that girl drama again. I mean, why don't females just understand that if they just played it cool, we'd want them? We're the males. We're the ones that want to conquer. If they just give it up and make themselves available, what the heck is fun about that? However, when they played games it was sort of annoying. I'm not saying that Savoy was trying to mess with my head, but because she hadn't been all over me, I wanted to be all over her. *Call her, man,* I said to myself. When I dialed the digits, I braced myself for the fallout.

"Hey guy!" Savoy's friendly voice said before I could even say hello. "I was just praying for you."

Okay, there were a whole lot of things I expected Savoy to say, but that definitely wasn't one of them. She was praying for me? I had failed a little in that department. I hadn't gone to God on her behalf. But then again, maybe I had—wishing her the best in my mind and hoping she was well was prayer.

"Perry, are you there?" she asked in my silence.

"Yeah, lady. You just are something special, that's all. Thanks for the prayers," I said. Maybe her intervening on my behalf is what helped me get through that night, and in my gut I felt she helped save me. "So I want to take you somewhere special," I just came right out and said.

I mean, why be formal and make it difficult to talk? If she was down for that she would let me know. And she did. We set a date.

It seemed that forty-eight hours came too slow as I looked at myself all dressed up. I headed over to her place. When Savoy opened the door, she had on the cutest outfit: jeans, a red top with diamond adornments, and sandals. As I walked her to my car and opened the door, I said, "I don't know what it is. I don't know if it is because I haven't seen you in a while, but you are so gorgeous."

Now I am typically the kind of brother who doesn't play it straight. I didn't want to show all of my cards. I liked to keep a little something back so she didn't think she could rule me, but again, I didn't want to hold back with her. I agreed with her father: She was a gem, and I would treat her special. Savoy flashed her pearly whites at me as we drove to a gospel play at the Civic Center. I was a little nervous.

"So this surprise date, where are you taking me?" she asked.

I smiled and pointed to the billboard advertising *Treat Me Right Boy or I'm Out.* She smiled. "I hear this play is good and the music is off the chain. This is going to be great!"

It was weird because at intermission she wanted to go to the ladies' room, but I just couldn't let her walk by herself. I wasn't trying to act or anything. The feeling just came naturally. I just didn't want any brothers to see her alone thinking she was available and all, and though I hadn't said it, I knew I wanted her to date only me.

"You're so sweet. You didn't have to walk me," she said as she nudged my knee with hers, making my knee buckle slightly. She laughed.

She was just a cool girl all the way around. She was not uptight. Toward the end of the play, I saw tears streaming down her face. I remember being at a few movies with Tori when she became all emotional, wanting me to hold her and show her some kind of affection. I did, because I wasn't up for an argument, but it wasn't really coming from my heart. I could not explain why I had just gently taken Savoy's hand and brought her palm to my lips and kissed it softly. She didn't even look at me. She just smiled and wiped the tears from her face with her free hand. Later in the car, she complimented me.

"You've been really over-the-top nice tonight, Perry, and I don't want you to think I'm high maintenance or anything. Now don't get me wrong, I love to hear you tell me I'm pretty, and hold my hand in public and be my escort, but you don't have to do any of that. I know there are no strings with us."

"What if I said I wanted there to be strings?" I said as I pulled into the country club parking lot where the Augusta National Golf Club Master's tournament was played. It was too cold to get out of the car, but just being in that serene place allowed us time to open up to one another.

"What are you saying? What do you want?"

"A relationship with you."

"I just got out of a relationship. You got school and senior stuff ahead. You have to get ready for college. I mean, you don't need to be tied down to one female right now."

I couldn't believe what she was saying. All the right words that a brother would want to hear. She was allowing me time to just be free and hang out and still be able to get with her. But I wasn't so eager to give her the same freedom. I didn't want to talk anymore. I just leaned in and kissed her.

"You don't need to look out for me," I said after we pulled apart. "I'm a big boy. I know what I'm doing."

"Don't get me wrong. I want you to commit to me. I want a relationship with you too, but right now you shouldn't have to be focused on one girl."

"Do I need to kiss you again? Or did you get my point? If you don't want to have me as your guy then I respect that."

She leaned in, kissed me and said, "Then if you want to be my man, keep making me feel the way you did tonight, and we will never have any problems."

Getting her home right at the time her father asked me to, I had no regrets signing up to be her boyfriend. I just hoped that in the morning my feelings would not have changed.

The next day was Super Bowl Sunday, and I had a little shindig over with my boys. Damarius, Cole, and Jordan came over as soon as I got home from church. I knew Cole chugged beer every now and then, but he was cool with the fact that all I was offering was soda. Jordan was just happy to be in the house, hanging out with us, the football players. He felt it was increasing his style, and I wasn't the one to argue with him anymore. He was cool. Not every athlete is a dumb jock, so having friends that were academically off the chain was fun. I looked over at Damarius going through my refrigerator.

He was all fidgety and antsy-like. He looked as if he wanted to ask me something, but he didn't know how.

"Naw, man, that unopened bottle in that refrigerator is my mom's."

"All right, all right Perry. So look. I got issues. I need to talk to you anyway."

He came at me like I was some psychiatrist or something.

"I need your advice, man. Actually I was advised to seek your counsel."

Now I really didn't understand what in the world he was talking about. I got a little close and sniffed his breath. I didn't smell anything.

"Man, have you been smoking?" I asked before realizing that was a place I did not want to go. Just as quickly I had said the words, I wished I could stuff them back in my mouth. "You know what, man? You grown. I'm gonna leave you alone," I quickly said, like a worm trying to wiggle off the hook.

"Naw, naw," he said, grabbing my shirt. "Jaboe wanted me to talk to you."

Oh, this was too much.

"Talk to me. What? Whatcha mean?"

"I owe him some money, Perry."

"Yeah, I heard him talk about you in debt. Pay him back."

"Man, I owe him four grand."

"What!" I wanted to slap him upside his head.

"I don't know, man. I'm starting to hear you. I'm gonna mess up my own chances. We're right in the middle of basketball season, and I swear sometimes I just get so tired, I be wanting to take my ownself out of the game. But I don't need to because maybe that's my only shot to get to college. Jaboe gave me an hour. He told me to talk to you. He said you were a wise brother, and you'd tell me the right thing to do. How can I kick this habit I got, man? Should I just walk away from my debt? You think Jaboe is going to be cool with that?"

This was crazy. Jaboe knew that I had to tell Damarius to stick with him or he'd release the video. And I pretty much agreed anyway to back off the situation. Why he had to stick my guy to me?

"Come on man. Just tell me again: 'Walk away, Damarius.' Say it out loud now. I guess I just need a little positive pushing. What's up, what's up?"

This was all getting a little cloudy in my brain because my inner soul was saying: *Forget yourself, man. You better save your boy.* And then there was my carnal side saying: *Ahh, heck naw, don't be no fool. If that tape get out, boy, your career will be over before it begins. Damarius gotta be smart enough for himself.*

"You gonna tell me something?" he cut in, interrupting my thoughts.

Neither side was winning the argument in my head. I just said, "Man, I'm going to watch the game."

He followed me into the living room, saying, "Man, come on and talk to me. Tell me something."

But I just waved him off and turned up the TV like I just had to see the Super Bowl pregame show. It was just a cover-up for me to see the Falcons and the Raiders in the big dance. Even though I had not pushed him toward Jaboe, I hadn't stopped him either. Wasn't that just as wrong? I needed to get a hold on all of this, but I was too embarrassed to ask the Lord for help. It was my stupidity that had gotten me in this position. I knew deep down that I could come to God with anything at anytime, but my pride wouldn't allow me to go there. I was really trippin'.

I hated seeing my character get out of order. I mean, what could I really do? I was caught between a rock and a hard place. It wasn't that I wanted to steer my friend wrong. He knew what he should and should not be doing. Four thousand dollars in debt to some thugs. He needed to find a way to pay Jaboe or it was very possible that he wouldn't stay standing.

"What's going on between the two of y'all?" Cole asked.

"Just trying to get some advice from my boy, man. He's ignoring me. I just can't understand it. Any other time Perry dying to tell somebody what to do. Now when I ask him for his two cents, he's quiet."

I listened to the two of them talk about me as if I were not there. Thankfully Jordan cut in on their conversation.

"Come on y'all, We supposed to be watching the football game. This is y'all sport. The Super Bowl. Y'all talking about advice and stuff? That's crazy."

"Thank you." I said.

"All right, all right. I'm sorry," Damarius replied as he finally sat down and we started watching the game.

I didn't understand how Damarius couldn't know what I'd really tell him to do. Leave the drugs alone. I mean why did he need somebody to push him to do right? Nonetheless, that was the case and I didn't step up to the plate because of my own selfishness.

We spent the next hour watching the game but I couldn't focus on it. If there were a mirror right in front of me, I couldn't have looked at myself in it. I wasn't a real team player and I guess it was eating me up. I needed to get this situation under control. Get it together. But the problem was, I had no clue how.

They were all into watching the last minutes of the Falcons and Steelers play. Even though the dirty birds had never won the championship, I still couldn't get into it like my boys. When they won, screams filled the room. However, I was struggling with my own issues too much to cheer. They were such great spectators that they didn't even realize I wasn't that into the game.

As my boys got up to leave my place after the game, Damarius stared at me. "Well, I guess it's okay what I'm doing. You didn't tell me it wasn't."

I just smiled.

"So then that's my answer. I can just keep doing what I'm doing. Work it out with Jaboe. It's not going to hurt me."

"Boy, you so silly. G'on and get outta here."

"Ohhh. I see what you doing. You want me to figure this one out on my own, huh? I respect that, Perry. You've been listening. Not trying to dictate and all that and being self-righteous. All right, all right. We gonna pick this up again."

"You don't need me in your life like that, man. You got it."

We slapped hands and I shut the door. I banged my head up against it a couple times. I truly hated that I couldn't do the right thing. The Christian thing. I guess I just wasn't there yet.

January thirty-first was my mother's birthday. After I worked out with my boys, I headed to the mall. I went in several stores but I couldn't find the perfect gift for my mom. Just getting something nice for her wasn't going to get it. I had a credit card with a thousand dollar limit and a three hundred and fifty dollar balance. So cost wasn't an issue for me. I just wanted a gift that would mean something special. I guess this is what I get for shopping last minute 'cause I couldn't find anything. I needed help.

So I turned to God. *All right Lord. You know she's real special. I just want to make her smile.* My mom had a track record of returning my gifts. When I was little that really didn't matter, but as I got older, and I took time to choose something I thought she'd really like and then she took it back, I was offended. Maybe that was why I'd waited until her birthday to shop for her gift. I was really dreading making a choice. After my short prayer I thought about Savoy. Heck, she was a girl with class. Maybe she could at least point me in the right direction. I dialed her number.

"Hey you!" she said, as friendly as always. That's what I was talking about. Just hearing her sweet voice sent jolts up my spine. Boy did I wish she was here with me—not just because I needed help with my mom's present, but because I wanted one more of those juicy kisses we shared a couple of weeks back.

"Perry, you okay?" she asked.

"Yes," I said as I hesitated, trying to figure out a way to ask her the question.

"You know we can talk about anything, Perry. What's up?"

"I mean, it's nothing heavy. It just seems sort of silly."

"What?"

"My mom's birthday."

"Ahhh. For real? That's so sweet."

"It's last minute. I'm trying to get her a gift. I called to ask for your help, and I know you're probably busy. But I'm in the mall and I can't even figure out what to buy her."

"What's the budget?"

"Under three hundred is cool."

"Ohhh. Dang, you got much money."

"Nooo. It's just a card. A quarterly allowance from my pops. So if I spend less that's better for me, but I mean, you know. I wanna get her something nice. Any ideas?"

"My mom and I have favorite designer label. It's called Brightened. Really classy purses, belts, luggage, watches, sunglasses."

"Where can I find it?"

"One of the department stores in there. I'm sure you'll find something in accessories."

"She needs a new purse. But she's not into the designer thing."

"That's what I love about Brightened. It doesn't display the name or anything like that. It just looks really sharp. You'll find a style that's *her* between two hundred and two hundred and fifty dollars."

"Yeah? Cool. So when we getting together again? I don't want to see you just on Valentine's Day."

"I sort of wanted to talk to you about that."

"What? Us going out again?"

"Nooo. Valentine's Day, silly. I wanna double date with my girl."

"Double date?"

"And I don't want you to say no. Just think about it."

I remembered Savoy's girlfriend. She went with us on the Christian retreat last year. She was a little flirty and I knew if I stepped to her door of opportunity, she'd bust it wide open.

"I'm not sure if that's a good idea," I said.

"Well, she's going to be going out with my brother."

"Oh heck no! You want me to double date with Sax? No, no, no, no, and no. If I look at you too hard, he'll be all over me. I'm just not down with that, Savoy. Come on, I wanna treat you to something nice. We just started our thing. I don't want us to have any distractions."

I needed to be clear with her about my intent. I wasn't down with the double date thing. I'd been there and done that with my boys and their girlfriends for years. Besides, Saxon and I wouldn't have anything to say to each other.

"Well, you guys are going to be going to the same school next year—well, maybe."

"What do you mean maybe?" I asked. Apparently she knew something I needed to know.

"I don't know. Saxon said something about a coaching change. A possible coaching change, and he might not go there next year."

I hadn't heard anything like that. I needed to start paying more attention to what was going on with my future school.

I knew that the head coach at Tech was under some pressure, but I hadn't heard any rumors of him being dismissed. Talking to Saxon on the side would be a good idea.

"I need to call your brother. Or better yet, tell him to call me."

"Cool, cool, cool. You guys need to be friends."

"Oh. I'm in the accessories section. These purses are dope."

I picked out a sassy brown and black one with silver detail for my mom. Recently, she changed all her jewelry to white gold. So I knew she would appreciate this gift.

"I'm lifting you up," Savoy said sweetly.

"I know you are, girl. I'm praying for you too."

"And Perry." She paused.

"Yeah?"

"I don't trust myself alone with you. That's really why I want to do the whole double date thing. Just you think about it."

Now she was shooting her feelings straight at me. I had to respect that.

"Truth be told," I told her, "I can't get you out of my head."

After getting my gift wrapped in customer service, I headed home and thought about Savoy's comment. I needed to step up and be the leader in our relationship and not make her feel like our being alone together would be too much for her. Oh, I knew I had to be real with myself. Sometimes when I looked at her I peeled off all her clothes in my mind. Would my impure thoughts be reflected in my actions? The Word says: "So as a man thinketh, so is he." *Lord, you gotta just help me to toughen up. I want to do the right thing. I need help.*

Tori's car was parked outside my driveway when I returned home. It completely interrupted my prayer because I had not invited her over. When I went inside, she was settling down with my mom in the dining room sipping tea.

"Hey babe!" my mom yelled as soon as I walked in the door. "Look at Tori. She remembered my birthday. She brought me flowers. Is that not sweet?"

I handed my mom my present from behind my back and kissed her on the cheek and said, "Yea, that's real cool." What was Tori up to? She and my mom had a nice relationship when Tori and I were dating. But her remembering my mother's birthday was not something I expected.

"We were talking for a while and now I'm going to go and open my present and let you two talk," my mom said.

Okay, now it's like my mom was pushing me toward working things out with her.

"Tori, it was really good seeing you, sweetie. You're a good girl," Mom said as she left the room.

I didn't like this one bit. I hadn't wanted to call it out in front of my mom. That would be rude. But I had to be honest.

"What are you doing here?"

"You don't want to sit and talk to me?"

"Naw, I have some homework. Answer the question."

She stood up and took my hand.

"I care about you and your family. Your mom's birthday has been on my calendar for the last two years. You know I was going to remember. I did something last year for her. I did something the year before. She's my friend, and she thinks we're good together."

I couldn't deny what Tori was saying. My mom had always liked her. But she didn't know all that I knew either. That the girl was on the verge of committing suicide sometimes. Over me. My mom would hate that. She's got a daughter. She definitely doesn't like weak women. That's why the time I caught her crying when she'd found out about my dad's affair, she was disgusted with herself because she didn't want me seeing her breaking down.

I hadn't told my mom all that I knew about Tori. I hadn't told her that I had broken up with her and that I'd even found a new girl. Since my mom liked Tori, she might be sort of over the top about a new girl. Once and for all I had to make sure Tori understood that we were through. Done. I'd committed myself to somebody else, but I didn't want to be a jerk about it. So I looked her in the eyes.

"Listen, I don't want to hurt you."

"Then don't. We can work this out. We can work through it."

"No, Tori. You need to hear me. I got another girlfriend now."

"Who is this chick?"

"You don't know her. She doesn't even go to our school."

"Well then I'll forgive you for that."

"Forgive me for what? We're not together. Come on, Tori. That's what I'm saying, babe."

"You called me babe. You care."

"Ahh. See, you tripping. I really like her. She's not clingy. She's smart. She's beautiful. She's headed off to college next year too, and she doesn't pressure me. Tori, we are over. I don't want you to break down on me. I want us to be friends. But if you keep popping up unexpectedly and keep taking what I say and twisting it around to convince yourself that I still love you, then I'm going to have to pull back for real. If you really do care about me—"

"I love you," she interrupted.

"—respect my decision that I have moved on. Show me you can do that."

"Okay. We're being honest and I'm not going to fall apart, but this hurts. I hear you though, Perry. But thanks for getting me straight."

~ 4 ~

Rethinking My Decision

A week later . . .

"Perry, get down here now, son," my dad yelled at the top of his voice. I didn't know what was going on. I didn't know whether somebody was sick, hurt, or dying. He had such urgency in his voice.

"Yes sir," I said, a little out of breath and agitated.

"Look boy. Look there at the TV."

We both sat there in silence staring at the newscaster report the firing of the Georgia Tech head coach. I sat there and watched the athletic director take a press conference on the matter, but I didn't hear a word he said. Everything I'd committed to was now ripped from under my feet. I felt like I was on my tail, wondering whether I should give up on Georgia Tech and start my search all over again. Then my dad spoke up. He said everything I wanted to say.

"See that's why those schools, man, they don't care about the players sometimes. They are doing what they think they need to do. It doesn't matter whether a kid or athlete commits to a particular coach. I know it is frustrating for you, and if you'd rather go somewhere else, we can look again. You've been recovering well, son. Thankfully that ligament you tore in the championship game is almost healed. I know there'll be tons of schools that would want you if they know you're available," he assured me.

"I just can't believe nobody called us," I finally said as I sat down beside my dad, sort of wishing I was eight again so he could hold me and tell me everything was going to be okay.

To anybody out there that wasn't into college sports, it seemed like no big deal that the school was hiring a new coach, but my dad and I knew different. I felt that he understood my agony when he placed his hand on my knee and patted it. It wasn't the hug that the boy in me needed, but the man that I was now appreciated the gesture. If they got rid of the head coach then more than likely the whole coaching staff would be gone. Not only did the old head coach promise me major playing time on his field, but the wide receiver coach had been drafted in the second round back in the day. Though he hadn't completed his rookie season 'cause he blew out his knee, he obviously had talent.

"You two look like the hail has damaged your cars."

Mom knew our minds had been on something. She had a great sense of humor and knew how to change the mood when things didn't seem right. She smiled and walked over to me and hugged me and told me she loved that purse. My dad complimented me and told me I had great skills in choosing what she liked. He told me that as long as he kept the green coming, she was happy, but that ever since I gave her the purse, she hadn't stopped talking about it. That my gift was a hit made me excited. I wanted to go call Savoy to tell her about it, but I sensed my parents wanted to say something to me.

"Y'all want to say something? I just want to go think about the school thing and maybe take my girlfriend out for some ice cream."

"So you and Tori got back together?" my mom asked with excitement.

"No, no-no-no-no. Mom that has been over. We're through."

"Well, who is she then?" Dad asked.

"The girl you went to the retreat with?" my mom questioned.

"Yes, that's her."

"And her brother plays ball? I saw that cute girl. I thought y'all had something going on," my dad added.

"Savoy Lee is her name."

"Well, sweetie, you don't have to take her out for ice cream in January," my mom said.

"It's February now, honey," Dad said.

Who cares if eating ice cream in February was a bad thing? If Savoy was up to it, I was for it. But maybe I wouldn't be the best company, I thought, what with my future thrown off course.

"Naw, I don't need to go nowhere," I said to my folks.

Surprised at my comment, Dad said, "Naw, son. You gonna be all right. Go on and clear your head. Get out the house for a bit and drive around in that nice ride. Go on out there and advertise your daddy's car lot so I can make some more sales this month."

My mom grabbed a pillow from the sofa and bopped him with it. I loved to see the two of them play with each other, especially when he pulled her into his lap. I smiled. This was the mom and dad I enjoyed and was used to. Last semester my parents argued and fussed all the time. I was glad that those old parents were gone.

"Son, you gonna be okay though. We're gonna find the right school for you."

"How you know he's gonna leave Tech?" my mom asked.

"They couldn't even call and let the boy know they were getting rid of the coach? Or maybe they didn't know."

"No, Mom. I heard rumors about it. Savoy heard about it from her brother."

"So why didn't you tell me?"

"I mean, it was just a rumor. She shared it with me yesterday and I actually forgot it."

About an hour and a half later, I was sitting in Shoney's waiting for Savoy to arrive. We met in Augusta, about half way between our houses. When Savoy came in with rosy cheeks from the cold, I stood up and hugged her.

"I'm surprised you called. My dad, Saxon, and I were going through Saxon's original list of schools to decide where he would go."

"Yeah, me and my dad talked about it. He told me that I needed to just go clear my head. I told my folks about you."

"About me?"

"Yeah. I got a girlfriend now. That's the only reason why I was able to leave the house. I told him I wanted to come out and meet you. First he thought you should pick me up, but my mom got onto him. He tries to talk to me about being independent, but then he wants to try to get others to do things for me. We have school tomorrow so we both know we can't stay long."

"Yeah, I just want some ice cream. One of those hot fudge sundaes. I just got a taste for it for some reason."

"That'll work. But you're shivering. You don't need any ice cream."

"The fudge is heated up here. Plus, it's girl time for me. You're my boyfriend. You should understand that I get a little moody sometimes."

"All right, that's a little too much."

"No it's not. I want you to understand me. I do get a little moody, I must confess, around this time of the month."

She was so cool. She reminded me of Payton. Tori never shared that kind of information. Savoy didn't appear to be moody. I just loved that she was so open. I took her hands as we sat across the table from each other.

"I just don't know what to do," I said. "All I wanted to do was to go to Georgia Tech and now because things have changed there, I don't know. It is really bothering me. This is my future. It's my life. But you don't want to hear about all that."

"No, this is a big deal. Like I said, my brother and father are sitting at home trying to analyze this and if you want my help to sort out what's best for you, I'm down with talking about it."

"What the heck did I do to deserve a girl like you? Dang," I said as I reached over and planted a juicy one on her check. "I appreciate that."

"I told you as long as you treat me right, we will have no drama."

"So then tell me. What do you think I should do? What is your brother doing?"

"I think I've told you a couple of times before. He's trying to figure it out right now. But this isn't about Saxon. What's best for him might not be best for you."

"But you're going to Tech. If you're going to be running track there, I want to be in the stands cheering for you just like you would be cheering for me."

"But this isn't about me either. If you and I can't connect at Tech, we can still work it out from anywhere. Just because they got a new coach you shouldn't up and change your mind. You gotta meet the new man. Figure out if his game plan fits yours. Sometimes schools get rid of people because they weren't producing."

"Yeah, but Tech was at .500. It's a doggone academic

school. It's not like they are going to win a national championship every year."

"No, but there's nothing wrong with the alumni wanting them to, and if you go to another school who's to say they won't get rid of your coach the next year or your junior year."

"So basically what you're telling me is no school is safe. Tech or anywhere else."

"Sort of. I think what I'm trying to say is that you will be a great asset to any school, Perry Skky Jr."

"Hmph, nobody ever calls me by my full name."

"You're smiling so I see you like it."

"Baby, I like it when you call me anything." I said.

She leaned forward and kissed me with her soft lips. As we waited on the hot fudge sundaes she continued.

"Sometimes, Perry, when you study too hard or over-study, you know, when you think too hard, you think wrong. Your first thought is usually the right one. Now, I don't know. I'm not saying Tech is perfect. I just know that whether you go to Tech or any other school, as long as it's on that same caliber, you'll rise to the top and no coach can keep you down, and no offensive scheme can keep you back. I watched my brother play for years and I thought he was the best at his position, but I've seen your tapes. I've seen your moves. You're the best wide receiver I've ever seen, and he gets mad at me when I tell him that. Bottom line: You'll be fine wherever you go. Enjoy the process of making the decision all over again."

I held her hand again and grabbed it really tight. She looked into my eyes and could tell that, though there were a lot of things I was confused about, being her man was not one of them.

The next couple of days I took the time to look at every college that had ever sent me a letter of interest. Though it was somewhat overwhelming, I knew it was necessary. My mom was helpful. She separated all the schools that I had shown an interest in from the ones she'd like and the ones my dad thought I needed to check out.

To get my mind right in order to make the best decision for me, I prayed. I asked the Lord to help me not get frustrated, and because I included him in the process, I was actually enjoying reconsidering my choice.

It wasn't until I went to work out with Cole and Damarius, my buddies, that I was able to see what was obvious. As I did curls on my strained leg, Cole kept count. Damarius blurted out something from another exercise machine.

"I just don't get why you won't look at the schools that were your top choices. The ones you visited before. I mean, did you just completely rule them out or were they just second to Tech?"

"Dang, boy, you might be on that stuff," Cole joked.

I definitely didn't want him to go there. I had purposely avoided what's been up with Damarius. What decision he'd come to. Where things stood with him and Jaboe. After doing an extra five curls, I spoke up.

"Naw, naw, naw. Wait. Don't rag on him. He's got a point. Keep talking D. Tell me what you thinking."

"Well I'm just saying you going back through every school. But there's gotta be a reason why you didn't look at them too seriously a couple of months back."

"Right, right, right," I said.

"So I'm just saying. You visited Miami. You visited Duke. You even went to Georgia, and I think since Payton goes there that's one of the schools you said you didn't want to go to. I don't even know why you ruled out the other two personally."

"Well, I mean Duke was *too* academic, and in Miami—the guys I hung out with were just trying to get their groove on."

"And what's wrong with that?" Damarius said.

"Ha-ha-hee-hee." I faked a laugh before standing up and bopping him upside the head. "You know I'm trying to go play ball and not girls."

"Yeah, man. But Miami is always competing for a national championship."

"Right, right. But they got too many stars. I might be on the bench all day."

"And that scares you? You supposed to be the man. Work it out. Claim your spot."

"And what's up with Duke though?" Cole asked.

"You smart and stuff."

"Again, I'm trying to go play ball, and I ain't talking about basketball."

"Maybe if you get on the team," Damarius suggested, "things would change."

I looked at Damarius and Cole and then stared straight ahead, thinking as I sat on the workout bench. Maybe I had judged those two schools unfairly. I definitely loved the campus at Duke, and its tradition, and the coach was pretty cool too. Could I be the one who made a difference? Could I help them win? Could I help Miami? Was I scared of a little competition? Did I not truly believe in my own ability? I liked both of those schools. Why not give them another chance? I looked at my boys again. I heard what they had said. They were seriously helping me work out so that I'd be ready to play in the fall season. Not only was the workout kicking my tail, but I also felt a little bad that with all Damarius was going through, he was being a better friend to me than I was to him. Somehow I had to change that.

My folks were happy to go with me to visit Duke and Miami. The first time I had gone by myself. Maybe this time having their wisdom to guide me, I'd see a different side. Sometimes, I used to think I knew it all, but it was coming down to the wire. In a week I would have to declare which university I wanted to attend. I was afraid that my knee injury and the fact that I had previously declared for Tech would mean that other teams wouldn't be interested in me. But thankfully that wasn't the case at all. We went to Duke University first. I don't know if it was the time of year or if the place was always this beautiful. My mom couldn't stop talking about how much she wanted me to go there. Sitting in the head coach's office, he laid it on pretty thick.

"I'm just going to be honest with you son. The world doesn't know us for winning championships in football. But I've been hired not to just bide my time and get a paycheck, but to make a difference in this program. I've filled all my spots but one, and I'm more than confident that if you come here, we'll build this program around you. We'll turn some heads in this game. You'll stand out every week and I think we can really shake some things up in the ACC. Look how tall you are. No one can guard you. Look how physically built you are. It's hard to tackle you. You are so quick, defensive backs can't even catch you. You take a chance on Duke University and you will not regret it."

I had to stop for a minute and think. What he was saying got to me. I mean, what was wrong with them building a program around me? I don't know. Maybe this was the place for me. Later that night at dinner, I was glad I didn't have to make a decision. We went to dinner with the wide-receiver coach and his wife, and two players, John and Tatey.

John Morgan was the outgoing wide receiver, and he told me that he wished he had my skills coming into college. I appreciated that. Most dudes I knew weren't about giving up props. He was real. He told me that he loved his education here and though he wasn't going to play professional football the school had equipped him with the skills and degree he needed to pursue anything in business. Then there was this freshman named Tatey Obama. He was a defensive back and said that I would help him increase his game if I came to the school.

"What's your reservation about coming here?" John asked me.

"Honestly, last time when I looked, I mean, it was just too academic for me. I mean, I'm a smart brother, but I do want to have a little fun in college. Plus, I wasn't sure y'all wanted to win here."

"Oh. So it's like that. We've got to hook him up."

As soon as the dinner was over, the coach and my parents went back to the players' lounge and talked some more. John and Tatey took me to three hoppin' parties. Not only did they fill me in on the latest news about the lacrosse team scandal, but they showed me that they just weren't all about the books. It was a side of Duke that I hadn't seen, and the town, though it was a college place, had a serious rocking atmosphere. All and all, I was glad I tried it out one more time. Certainly, some of the things that had swayed me against choosing Duke, I now saw differently, and I was thankful for that.

The next day, we immediately flew south to Miami. This time I was picked up in a limousine and driven straight to the head coach's house and he too laid on a thick pitch. I tried not to be overwhelmed when I was greeted by seven of their best players, all the offensive coaches, and the athletic director.

"I brought the best to my house today to show you that you can stand with them," the head coach announced.

"I don't know, coach. He might be too much of a mama's boy," one of the players called out, and the others laughed.

My mom defended me. "But he still can take care of business."

It was interesting. I didn't want her defending me, but

hey, I knew I was her heart. So what could I say? As I looked around the room at some of the best players in college football, I had to ask myself questions. Did I not think I was just as good? Wouldn't being around them day in and day out help to elevate my game even more? Then the coach interrupted my thoughts and broke it down for me.

"Son, your dad called us and said you were reconsidering your choice of university. Everybody here in this room is committed to winning and we all feel that you are the key to help us grab the national championship. We can do it next year. We can do it all four years that you are here. That's our goal. We just need to know if you are on board with us or not."

Was that a question that I was supposed to answer right then? I was dumbfounded.

"All right, I'm catching you a little off guard. But I hope that if the quarterback throws you an unusual play that you're ready for it."

"All right, coach. I'll be ready."

"So what's your hesitation?"

"Oh, he loves this school, sir," my father said.

He would be very happy if I became a Hurricane.

"Bruce, Carlos, y'all show this young man our great school and city," the coach said.

Bruce White was an upcoming senior and the best offensive tackle in the country. Carlos Young was the third running back. A sophomore. I was actually surprised when we got in the car and Bruce said, "I can't hang out with you too much, young blood. I got a big exam this week." I just don't know why I thought the players wouldn't be focused on academics. But here was the best defensive tackle in the country talking about exams. I asked them questions about the school's academic programs for the next twenty minutes and they gave me the run-down about the school's statistics. Though they were in the Athletic Coast Conference, they were a private school. Academic standards here were higher than I initially thought. Bruce touched base with the head coach to see how our schedule was going, and the next thing I know, Bruce took me to visit the Dean of the School of Business. After I finished talking to the dean, I knew Miami would give me a run for my money academically if I decided to go there.

Now I was really torn. I liked Duke. I liked Miami. My mom sensed I was stressed over my choices as we flew home to Augusta on the private jet that Miami had arranged for us.

"Son, any school you go to can prepare you to succeed. You just got to look at it with a positive attitude and recognize all the opportunities."

"Yep. Your mother's right. You know that old adage. Quit looking at that glass half empty, boy. Just pick a school and run with it," my dad added.

Mom was right. I had to keep positive about this whole thing. So as I got home that night from a weekend of college visits, I prayed and gave it all to God.

~ 5 ~

Finalizing the Dream

Coach Lincoln Red, new head football coach at Georgia Tech, would be at my house in less than ten minutes. I knew that he was going to be on time, but for some reason I just couldn't get myself ready for the meeting. He'd been at the school for what, a week? But he hadn't reached out to me until now. He had probably got wind that I had been visiting certain schools and now all of a sudden I was a high priority.

"Son, hurry up," my dad said as he came into my room. I just gave him one those looks, a stare only a father could understand.

"All right. I feel you," he said as he entered and shut the door. He pulled out the chair from under my computer desk, turned it backwards, and sat down. I guess he called himself trying to be cool.

"You're thinking it's too little too late. Right, son?"

"Yeah, Dad. I mean, I don't even know why I said I'd go."

"You chose Georgia Tech for a number of reasons and the old head coach was only one of them. I gotta admit, I think the University of Miami is the best choice. But your mom likes Duke, so hey, maybe your choice is the right one for you, son."

"What do you mean?"

"The choice you made before. Your choice to go to Tech. I mean, I don't know. Maybe you should go there. We at least owe it to this whole process to meet the guy."

"I mean, he could bail out of college coaching again and go back to the pro level."

"He failed at that. Lincoln Red is one of the best college coaches around. He tried the NFL thing, but he couldn't get those rich jokers to perform. So now he's trying to capitalize on some of that success he had in Alabama in the SEC and move on over to the ACC with a high profile school that really needs his leadership to win.

"So hurry up, boy. He'll be here in a minute, and you ain't gonna embarrass nobody. If you don't want to go to that school after this is all said and done, then we'll let him know. But for right now we accepted the meeting, and we're going to take it. Plus, the school's paying for dinner. You know I like spending somebody else's money," he said as he popped me upside the head and then turned my chair back under my desk.

"I can't believe I'm sitting at the table with Lincoln Red," Damarius said, seated to my left.

We had a private room at Augusta National, an exclusive country club where the golf tournaments were played. Coach Red didn't even live in Augusta but somehow he pulled off this high profile room and meal. At dinner were my mom, my dad, Coach, the new offensive coordinator, Damarius, and Cole.

We had followed him to the place so this was my first real interaction with Coach Red. He was a legend. I heard what Damarius was saying. My boy respected the coach in front of me. Deep down I guess a part of me did too. I grew up watching him take the University of Alabama to two consecutive national championships. I remembered his speech on ESPN when his quarterback won the Heisman, and I also remember the last three years when he was the head coach of the Washington Redskins when all the expectations they had for him going in, were never realized. Folks from up there couldn't wait to get him back to the college level, and Georgia Tech was happy to accept him. And why shouldn't they? His résumé was tight.

Other coaches had been known to lie about their qualifications. Some coaches, even before you could turn your head, were getting in trouble with the law. Coach Red had strong ethics. He wasn't changing grades for players. He'd been known to make sure most of his players graduated, and along the way, if they couldn't cut it in the classroom, he wouldn't allow them to set foot on the field. Yeah, Coach Red was a coaching legend. But sitting before me, he seemed a little cocky, like he didn't need to sell himself to me. Like I should just think he was all that. I mean, dang. He wanted *me* to sign with *him*. I had other opportunities, and I don't know, maybe I had a little pride thing going on as well.

The offensive coordinator did a lot of talking over dinner. My mom's head was nodding in approval and my dad voiced his agreement. I was trying to be skeptical of the bull. How did I know if they were planning to use me in their scheme like I wanted to be used? Observing Coach at the table, I could tell he could see I was still reluctant to buy into what I was hearing. So he spoke up.

"Well, you know. You all keep talking. I think I'm going to step outside with Mr. Perry here. That's okay Dad, right? We can have a little man-to-man talk."

Looking at Coach Red, I was as surprised as everyone else was. I wasn't expecting him to want to rap to me. But at least now it was going to be my chance to see for real where Lincoln Red stood when it came to Perry Skky Junior.

"All right, so let me be straight with you, son," he said, standing close to me.

Coach Red was all in my grill. I was backed up against some rails, and he had my full attention as he was standing firm and speaking calmly.

"I know you've been checking out other schools. You've probably been frustrated that I haven't given you the baby treatment. I know this thing all happened quickly, especially right around signing time too, and that's not fair. But son, life's not fair, and you're not the big fish in the small pond where I'm concerned. I'm trying to make sure that my current players can keep their grades up so they can play next year with you on the team. I've got some other kids. Two boys from Conyers. This guy from South Carolina that's a wide receiver. I'm trying to keep those guys on the team. I'm trying to bring in an offensive lineman from Tennessee and a defensive kid from Alabama. So though you're real good, I can stand to lose you, and I think I'll be okay. I know how to win," he said without hesitation.

No way did I want to appear weak. This coach couldn't ruffle me.

He continued in a softer tone. "You have talent, son. But do you think you know how to win on a college level? The coach that just left Tech won six games in a good year. Yes, he recruited you guys to come here, and I won't take that away from his staff, but what can he do with the talent? He's recruited good guys, but they hadn't produced on the field. You've got to get kids to play like a team and not see themselves as the stars of the team. If you come into my system, you'd be a team player, but you still will stand out. I will get you ready to play on the next level. I've played there myself, and I've coached there. I wasn't successful at the professional level because I had to learn where I was best, and for me, that's developing college players. You want the best for you? You want to meet your goal? Don't change your mind. Stick with Tech. And the little goals and dreams you have set for yourself, I promise, together son we'll blow those out of the water. You'll achieve greatness beyond your imagination. And if you ever want to have a chat with me, all you have to do is pick up the phone and call me. Don't wait for me to always make the first move. Got it?"

"Yes sir," I said, understanding and respecting him.

"Tech's your choice, right?" he questioned.

I just grinned.

"I like you, son. I'm confident that you will side with us. We'll have a letter ready for you on Tuesday."

As we went back into the dining room, his hand firmly on my back, I respected him for another reason. He helped me hone in on what I was truly looking for. Someone to believe in me seriously. Two hundred percent. To want more for me than I wanted for myself. Yeah, that's what I wanted in a coach, and Lincoln Red stepped up and laid it on the line and told me that's what he wanted to do for me. I knew I'd sleep on it a couple of days. But he was right. He had won me over.

The next day I was sitting in the back of church sort of chillin'. As a little kid, older ladies used to pat me on the head, looking at me as Payton's little brother. Now I was the big man. I filled my own shoes. I saw people whispering about me, deacons wanted to shake my hand, the pastor's wife would give me kisses on the cheek.

I could honestly see how this much attention could lead to an inflated ego. I knew I didn't need to pay attention to all the noise going on around me, even though the noise was about me. I needed to keep my focus on God. The pastor that I had been listening to for years stood and began speaking, and it seemed as if he was speaking directly to me.

"Have you had a dream? Something you felt God gave you? Planted deep inside your soul that was on the verge of happening, but stuff just kept getting in the way? So the dream couldn't be actualized as bright as you envisioned it? Anybody out there know what I'm talking about?"

A lot of "Amens" were spoken. I stayed quiet, but still tuned in. Where was he going with this thing? I picked up the church bulletin and the message read: The Answer's in the Tongue. What was he trying to say with that? So I listened in to find out.

"Sometimes you can do all the right things. Be in the right places. Pray hard. And sometimes even with all of that, things still don't work in your favor. Or maybe it don't work as smoothly as you think it should. Maybe that dream just isn't happening for you and you cry out: Lord, why? Why me?"

I could feel him then. I was with the pastor at that moment. Just when I had decided to go to Tech, they switched coaches, and I don't know what decision I might make. It could be the right one or the wrong one. The pastor continued.

"Sometimes you too scared to make any move at all. Fearful that whatever direction you move in—if you turn left or if you turn right, if you go with what's in front of you or what's at the back—you will go to the wrong place. Instead of telling yourself that you can, you start telling yourself that you can't. You start thinking you're the worst, instead of knowing you can make the right decision and say out loud: *I don't know what the heck I'm doing!* Are y'all following me now?"

The crowd nodded. The was a pause from the minister. I listened, waiting eagerly to hear the rest.

Finally he began again. "The tongue is the answer. Life and death are in the power of the tongue. Claim it. Speak God's word into existence for your life. Know that whichever way you decide to go, God will be with you. Ask Him to lead and guide you and to help you through. Tell Him you love Him even when things aren't going right. Praise Him when things are going wrong. Be excited about the good that you have and be just as pumped as when things go your way. See, we're not here for our own glory. I know we've got Perry Skky Junior in here set to sign a big college deal soon, and I don't even know what college he's going to, and I'm his pastor."

The church burst out laughing as the pastor smiled.

"Perry, you in here, son? I know you here."

People started pointing to me. I couldn't believe he was calling me out in the sermon. I raised my hand.

"Stand up, son. Stand up. Church, we want him to score many touchdowns so we can feel good. We all had a hand in raising this boy."

"That's right now. Tell the truth," Deacon James yelled out.

"Yeah. We all had a hand in raising him," one of the elderly ladies said.

"But church, his touchdowns are not to give this church glory or himself or his parents or his friends. His success in football and anything else is to give God glory, and God has put him where he is to succeed in drawing men unto the Lord. Perry, we wish you much success and let me see you after church. I want to know what school you have decided on. I don't want to have to find out on the news when you can share it with me right here. All right?"

"Yes, sir," I said and sat back down.

"Seriously, church. Our success is for God. He wants us to speak positive things into the air to give Him glory. To lift His name because that's how He gets reverence, and that's how

He knows we adore Him. He can take care of any problem.
He can guide us through any situation. We can get through
anything with Him. We just have to say it's so. Can y'all say
that with me, church? 'It is so.'"

I felt myself saying under my breath: "It is so." But then he
asked again for us to say it louder, and I spoke it. I didn't
know if Georgia Tech was going to be the right place. Pastor
was right. I did have doubts about Duke, Miami, Georgia
Tech, and any school, but it didn't matter 'cause God was
going to go with me. I just needed to make a decision, and
know that it was going to work out just perfectly. No matter
how it played out. One touchdown or one hundred. God
needed to get the glory, and as long as I was about living my
life for Him then that's when it all could work out for me,
and what a great lesson to learn. I just prayed I wouldn't forget it, and I checked myself before going to see the pastor
after church. I told myself that I wasn't going to forget that
the answer was in the tongue. To achieve greatness, I had to
keep saying great things.

Two days later, it was the Tuesday of the national signing
day for high school football players. I was thrilled that my
parents were excited about my choosing Georgia Tech. Even
though my dad would have preferred that I choose Miami,
and my mom was partial to Duke, collectively they were thrilled
about my decision to stay at Tech. My father had called Coach
Red Monday morning and informed him. When coach and I
spoke on the phone his excitement was oozing through my
ear. I'll never forget his words.

"Son, you made the best decision possible. You'll never
regret going to Georgia Tech. We're going to have one heck
of a year. Now don't change your mind on me," he teased toward the end of our conversation.

Pulling up into the parking lot and seeing all the media

there—television and radio and newspapers—it really hit me that this was a pretty big day for me. As soon as I got out of my car, Cole grabbed me around my neck.

"Man, can you believe it? It's for you and me. All this. It's for you and me! Augusta ABC channel, CBS channel, and even the Atlanta Journal paper has somebody here. Somebody is here from Columbus too, man. I am so psyched. It's about us today, boy. We worked hard."

"Yeah, it's about y'all today. You want to do a little celebrating?" Damarius said in an overly sarcastic tone as he handed me a brown paper bag.

I snatched it from him.

"Boy, this is stupid. Why are you drinking in the middle of the morning?"

"Man give me that back! Give me that back!" he said, barely able to stand. "Don't be mad 'cause I want to celebrate my two best friends going off to college." His words slurred, making it hard to make out what he was saying. I didn't know where his attitude was coming from, but I didn't like it, and I didn't like seeing him like this.

"Man, he's been like that ever since I picked him up this morning. I tried to tell him he didn't need to drink. But all he kept saying was that I didn't understand."

"You don't understand. Come on, Perry. Give me my bottle back."

"Dang, Damarius, what are you drinking?" I asked.

I sniffed the strong substance and knew it was some kind of liquor.

"Man, he got vodka," Cole said.

"It's clear. So teachers gonna think it's water. I started to take some rum from my dad's cabinet, but nobody ever sees me drinking tea. So that wouldn't work."

I grabbed him by his collar and pulled him toward the driver side of my car.

"All right, man. What's up with this? Why you acting like this? What's going down?"

All of a sudden, I saw news trucks coming toward me. Cole whispered, "Man, stop. They think you fighting him."

I didn't really care what people thought at that moment and this I needed to deal with. Damarius didn't need to be drinking and getting expelled from school. He was the star basketball player, graduation was right around the corner. He didn't need to mess things up for himself. I just had to be the bigger friend.

"Just take him over to the side. Let me talk to the media. Take him over to the side," Cole said.

So I dragged my friend around to the back of my car.

"What's going on? Why you acting like this?" I asked Damarius.

"As if you don't know, Damarius is the only one of the three musketeers that ain't going nowhere. Born and raised in Augusta. Gonna stay in Augusta. Nobody's given me a scholarship to nobody's college and I'm celebrating that too."

Oh, now I knew what was going on with him. He saw this day as a personal defeat or failure. I prayed quickly: *Lord, what in the world can I say to him? He's halfway out of his mind because of all this alcohol. I just don't know.* Something pierced my spirit as if it were a sword of knowledge coming straight from heaven. It hit my heart and poured out of my mouth.

"Look, man. My measuring stick is right here and yours is right there. What I do in my lane is my thang and what you do in yours is your thang. Don't get it twisted. It might seem like I'm getting ahead of you right now. But that's supposed to be cool because we're boys, right? You're supposed to be happy for me. But just because you don't have a contract today or a scholarship or whatever, it doesn't mean it's not coming tomorrow. You better at basketball than I ever could be in football."

"It's my grades though, man."

"And you can't get no knowledge into that brain all drunk. I got some coffee in my car. And I always keep some mints. Hold on. You gonna be straight, man."

"I am happy for you, Perry. I am," he cried. The alcohol was messing with his emotions.

Cole heard Damarius as he left from the media group and returned to the back of the car.

"Man, we know you proud of us. We proud of you too. You wouldn't have been pushing us all along, we never would've or could've gotten here."

"Never would've, never could've." I just had to laugh and joke with my friend. The three of us cracked up.

I looked at Damarius and said, "Man, seriously. Stay in your lane. You gonna make things happen for yourself."

"That's right. That's right. I am. Let's get y'all in here. So y'all can sign on the dotted line," Damarius sang as he did a crazy dance. He got in the car, drank the coffee, and grabbed some mints, and we all walked into the school. Cole and I went to the gym where the reporters were waiting. The principal had a letter of intent for me from Georgia Tech and one for Cole from South Carolina. It was great for us to put our names in ink saying we were committing to those schools. As we lifted our pens from the page, we heard a big cheer from the crowd, and from the back we heard Damarius yell.

"Those are my boys! Yeah!"

People started laughing. A part of me knew I was accepting this for the both of us 'cause Cole was right. We had been tight friends for a long time. I had gotten this far because I had boys that cared for and encouraged me. I looked over at Cole and said, "Man this is a good day."

Cole's mom came up and presented him his jersey from the University of South Carolina. Then my parents came up and gave me my jersey from Georgia Tech with my name imprinted on the back. Number 80. I was so excited. I got to keep my number from high school. As we enjoyed the hype, the principal spoke up.

"Okay. Okay. Coach. We've got one more announcement."

"Well, Perry. Would you come over here, young man?"

I stepped away from my parents and walked over to my high school coach.

"You have made a great impression on so many of us at Lucy Laney High School. You've been a leader on campus and off. You've soared academically and athletically. You've broken so many records here at our school. In the four years you have been here you've accomplished a lot. Though I only got the chance to coach you for one year, your record of sixty touchdowns is something special. I'm announcing now that in the fall season we plan to retire your jersey at our homecoming game."

The crowd went wild. I was speechless. I wasn't expecting it. Then the crowd chanted.

"Speech! Speech! Speech!"

"I don't know, man. I guess, I know y'all are more excited about being out of class than y'all are for this ceremony."

The crowd laughed.

"Naw, seriously. I just want to say anybody out there that has a dream, I stand up here for you. Dig deep inside yourself. I know it may seem tough sometimes, but know that you can succeed and that you can achieve greatness. Believe in yourself. I believe in God, and he's gotten me to this place.

"That's right!" somebody yelled out.

"And I just want to say to you guys that the things you work hardest at in life will bring the greatest rewards. Set goals for yourself. It don't matter how tough they are. Don't let anyone deter you from knowing you can make it happen. It's not just about seeing the dream, but it's about finalizing the dream."

~ 6 ~

Committing My Heart

Females are a trip, especially when it comes to Valentine's Day. I wanted to do something special for Savoy. I couldn't stop thinking about the girl. I knew she couldn't celebrate with me on my signing day because she had to be there with her brother, who committed to Georgia Tech too. When she told me that she wanted me to go on a double date with her brother and her best friend, Ellis, I was reluctant.

Saxon and I hadn't talked in a while. However, we were both in the Beautillion that my mom's sorority, Delta Sigma Theta, was sponsoring. But he was a cocky little something. Hanging out with him for a night like we were boys, I mean, I really wasn't feeling it. He had no problem letting me know that he was about dogging women, but yet he wanted to make sure he policed how I treated his sister. I was a better gentleman than he ever hoped to be.

Savoy's girlfriend, Ellis, was a trip too. Even if Savoy and I weren't officially dating, Ms. Ellis was not the type of girl I liked. Even though she'd be Saxon's date, I still think she might try to get with me, like she did when we went to the FCA retreat. Besides, women don't change when it's something that they really want, at least in my experience. I just am not up for problems in my new relationship. But hey, here I was being a gentleman and compromising because this was one thing Savoy wanted, and I wanted to be with her. So I agreed to go.

As I waited for the three of them to scoop me up from my crib, I reminded myself that I had to be on my best behavior, not look for trouble, and try to enjoy the evening for Savoy. I don't know if it was the newness of our relationship that I just wanted to keep it right, or if it was something else. But deep down, I knew I wanted it to last.

Today wasn't the prom or anything, but my parents acted like it was. They were right behind me ready to entertain my friends, and when they pulled up to my house, Mom was the first to welcome them.

All excited she said, "Y'all come on in! Come on in!"

The three of them got out of the car and walked in the door that my dad held open. I hoped my parents would chill out. Looking like I had overprotective parents was not the image that I wanted to portray.

"Ohh. She is so cute." My mom looked at Ellis.

"Mom, wait. That's Savoy's best friend."

I went and grabbed Savoy's hand. "This is my girl, Savoy."

"Oh my goodness. I am so sorry."

"I know honey. Trying to get our son in trouble," my dad teased.

I gave Savoy a kiss on the cheek. Couldn't believe I did that in front of my parents. That wasn't my normal style. I led Savoy over to the kitchen table and picked up the card and the bouquet of roses that I bought her and handed them to her. Savoy let out a cute, soft scream of excitement and gave me a hug.

"Yes, Savoy, my son bought them himself for you," my mom said proudly.

"That's right. Take care of my sister, man." Saxon called out.

"Saxon Lee," my dad said, "so you two are going to be in the same offense next year?"

"All of them are going to Tech, sir, except me," Ellis spoke up with a disappointed frown.

"Oh, Savoy, you're going there too?" my mom questioned in a nonchalant way.

"Yes ma'am. On a full track scholarship."

"Track? An athlete? Go girl!" my dad said.

"Yes, she's really good. My sister might make it to the Olympics one day, sir."

"Oh yeah. Now I see why my son wanted to go to Tech." My father smiled at Savoy.

Saxon and my father shared the laugh. My mom gave my dad the eye. He stopped.

"Y'all ready to go?" I said.

"Well wait. Not so fast," my mom said, "I want to see you give her the other gift that you bought."

"Perry, you got me something else?" Savoy asked.

"Dang, Ma. Can I have a little privacy?"

"For real, Pat," my dad agreed. "Don't let us keep you. Y'all go on out and have some fun."

"No, no. Mrs. Skky wants to see the gift. I want the gift too," my girl said boldly.

I looked at her, my mom and everyone else. Everyone awaited the gift. So I reached in my pocket, pulled out the small box, and handed it to her.

"Girl, the box is small," Ellis said.

"Don't be jealous now," Saxon called out to Ellis.

"Ha-ha-ha," Ellis said.

"So man, that's you?" my dad asked Saxon in what he thought was a low tone.

"No. He's not my boyfriend. He's too much of a playa," Ellis said as her eyes rolled.

"But y'all are going out on Valentine's Day? You like him," my dad teased.

"Ahh, Perry, why can't you be down like your dad. You know it pops. She all into this," Saxon boasted as he pointed at himself.

Savoy interrupted their side chatter. Once the paper was off the gift box everyone looked as she opened it. Inside was a white-gold necklace and matching bracelet.

"Ahhh, Perry. Thank you," she said as she bent over and gave me a sweet peck on the lips.

"Dang, sis." Saxon voiced.

Savoy defended, "It was just a thank you."

"Oh, she's fine," my mom responded, shocking me by approving of my girl.

We didn't get out of the house easy either. My dad took Saxon down to the basement and asked him all about his career. When they came up, it was like they were best buddies or something.

"Car dealership and stuff, sir? My dad has worked at the Savannah River Plant all his life. But I wish he had more . . . like you."

"Well, son, your dad has a respectable job."

"Yeah I know, I'm just saying, I really admire you and it comes from here," Saxon said as he pointed at his heart.

My dad said, "Man, I'm proud of you too, son. Best player in South Carolina. You gave my son a run for his money. I'm going to be cheering for you with your dad, and who knows, we might make a track meet or two, Miss Lady."

"And hey, where do you plan on attending school next year?" my mom asked Ellis.

"I'm thinking about Georgia or Albany State."

"Oh wow. My daughter's at UGA."

Ellis asked, "Really?"

"You know Payton. We met her last year," Savoy said to Ellis.

"Oh yeah. That's right," Ellis responded, and then turned and looked at me. She licked her lips.

My mom gestured for Savoy to follow her. She took Savoy to the kitchen with her to get something to drink.

I looked at Ellis eyeing me and said, "I'll be right back."

"No. No. Don't go anywhere. I just want to check you out for my girlfriend," Ellis said as she blocked my path.

I replied, "Trust me. If her parents think I'm cool, you don't have to check me out."

My words didn't stop her. She turned to see if the coast was clear. Then she shocked me. The girl started unzipping her sweater.

"What are you doing?" I asked in a disgusted tone.

"Oh. Come on, Perry. You're an athlete. I know you boys like to have your cake and eat it too, and Savoy and I are girls. We borrow a lot of each other's stuff. We even use each other's lipstick. What touches her lips touches mine."

"I thought you liked her brother."

"Saxon and I have an understanding. We have a little fun sometimes, but we're not mutually exclusive to each other. I saw the way you've been looking at me since I entered your parent's house."

"You've only been here twenty minutes and trust me, I've been turning my head all day because of the way you've been looking at me. Come on now, Ellis, move."

I was so frustrated. I backed up since she wouldn't, then I went around her and walked to the kitchen where my mom and Savoy were chatting. I did not want to be around that crazy girl. She was up to no good and in no way did I want to jeopardize what I had with Savoy.

I entered the kitchen and said, "Hey. I'm going to drive."

"Why?" Savoy said as she got up from the kitchen table.

My mom said, "Yeah sweetie, there's no need for you to drive if you guys are going to the same place, especially with how high gas is nowadays. Plus, sweetie, don't rush her off."

"Mom, it's Valentine's Day. I know you and Dad want to have a little alone time," I joked.

"Boy, quit being mannish, and I'm thinking the four of you all staying together is a good idea."

She just didn't know how wrong she was. I didn't feel like going into it more either. She was going to have to trust her son knew best. However, she stood with her hands on her hips demanding I explain.

Ready to get the heck up outta there, I said, "Well, I'm just saying. When our date is over, they won't have to drive all the way back over here. They all live in Augusta you know."

"Yeah, that's true," my mom said.

"Oh, I like this boy," my dad said when he and Saxon came back into the kitchen. They had been all over the place getting to know each other. It seemed to me that they were bonding a little too much.

Finally, my mom turned Savoy loose and my dad quit talking to Saxon so he and Ellis could walk out with us. I was thankful that we were leaving, but more importantly, I was thankful that Savoy didn't argue me down about driving in a separate car. I was glad that Savoy was in my ride and we were following Saxon and Ellis.

I was quiet on the drive and so was Savoy. I really didn't know what I was supposed to say. I didn't know if I should come clean about Ellis coming on to me, or if Savoy was testing me out. I mean, how can a girl come on so strong up in my crib with her girl right around the corner, and my mom and dad nearby too? Was Ellis messing with me? Testing or something? Either way I had to keep quiet. Savoy said she and Ellis were really close. I didn't want to mess that up.

"Why you so quiet?" Savoy asked me, breaking into my thoughts.

"I'm sorry. My bad. I don't know. I'm just driving. Following. You like the roses? The jewelry?"

"Oh. Perry. That's so thoughtful," she said with a sweet, thankful look.

All of a sudden my cell phone rang. I didn't know who it was. Besides, I was trying to be out on a date. So I decided to let it ring. Savoy picked it up and saw Tori's name flashing across the screen.

"Tori? That's the ex-girlfriend, right? You didn't drive so you can drop me off and hang out with her later tonight, did you?"

"Oh see. You got jokes."

"No, Perry. I'm serious."

"Come on, babe. You said you weren't all possessive and jealous and stuff. You know it's not like that."

"Okay, you don't have to be defensive. I'm just telling you how I feel. I hope we can be honest in our relationship."

"Okay, I'm sorry. I just don't want to be questioned. That's what threw me and Tori off. She just flipped on me. I don't know why she's calling. I told her I had a new girl," I sighed.

"It's cool," Savoy said as she started rubbing the back of my head.

I felt better. She wasn't saying anything. She wasn't shooting any bull. Her hand just let me know that she cared that I was stressed. She wanted me to calm down. I reached over and grabbed her hand. I brought it to my lips and kissed it gently. I could tell Savoy wasn't about playing games. I relaxed, looked at her, and smiled. She smiled back. I looked at the road and decided to change the subject.

"You know you told me a long time ago that you went out with the white dude because the brothers were trifling. You saw your brother running around and you thought he and every other brother were really up to no good, huh. I hope you think that I am different from that, right?"

She looked into my eyes and said, "Yes, with my whole heart, I sort of feel you're different from that."

"Sort of?" I said.

"Okay, I believe you're different."

All of a sudden, her brother sped crazily towards an abandoned gas station. We had to swerve quickly to follow.

"What's wrong with him?" Savoy screamed.

"Are you okay?" I asked my girl.

"I'm fine. It's just he makes me sick sometimes. He does stupid stuff," Savoy said, frustrated.

We weren't stopped thirty seconds before Saxon slammed the door and came over to my car, trying to open my door. He was pounding on it like he was losing his mind. My door was locked yet he kept yanking on it.

"What is wrong with you?" Savoy yelled.

He was saying something that neither of us could understand. I had to talk to him. Before I got out of my car, I saw Ellis exit Saxon's car all dramatically. Why was she running from his car, wiping her eyes and pointing at me? I didn't know what she had told Saxon, but by the way they both were acting, I knew it was a big fat lie. I got out of my car carefully, leaving the door open, and spoke to Saxon.

"Hey man. Calm down."

"Calm down? Calm down? How can I be calm? You trying to date my sister when you coming on to her best friend at your house. Plus she was out with me. You don't even respect that." Saxon turned his eyes toward Savoy and ordered, "Savoy, get out of the car."

She shouted back without moving, "No. What are you talking about?"

"Savoy. Get-out-of-his-car," Saxon slowly said to his twin sister.

"Savoy, stay right there," I said, wanting a chance to tell her my side. "Sax, why don't you just let me and you talk about this before you go getting all mad about stuff you hear."

Savoy did finally get out of the car, and she ran over to Ellis. I couldn't believe this. Now my girlfriend was going to get fed a bunch of lies. It seemed like there was nothing I was going to be able to do about it.

"Savoy, you don't know what he tried to do," Ellis said loudly.

I couldn't hear what Savoy said next and that frustrated me. I tried to head over in their direction, but Saxon held me back, grabbing me by my coat. I don't know if I was more ticked because he put his hands on me or that he was messing up my brand-new leather jacket.

"You need to let me go, Lee," I said, looking him square in the face, giving him a chance to take his hands off me.

"Oh. Oh. So what? You gonna feel up all on my girl and then when I try to do something with you, make you be accountable, you gonna try to get all tough with me?"

Before I could deck him, Savoy stepped between the two of us. "Sax, I saw her looking at Perry the moment we stepped into his mama's house. She just admitted to me how sorry she was. She was just trying to get a rise out of you by using Perry. She just said maybe you'd like her if you felt Perry did. And for some strange reason, my girlfriend doesn't want me to be happy either. So she practically offers it up to my new man and makes sure my brother hates him. Way to go, Ellis!" Savoy yelled.

I was shocked. I couldn't believe Savoy got to the truth like that. I mean, right before the whole crazy scene, I was trying to be real with her by letting her know I wouldn't try to hurt her. But it looked like she knew what type of friend she had. She got the point that I wasn't trifling like that. I was happy to get back in my car and leave the two nuts, Saxon and Ellis, standing there alone.

I hadn't driven too far when I looked over and saw Savoy in tears. At the same time a thunderclap roared from the sky. Over the radio came a severe thunderstorm warning for the area.

"Baby, are you okay?" I asked as I looked over at her.

"You just need to watch the road in this bad weather. Can you even see?"

Savoy was right. When I looked back at the road, the rain was falling so hard it was hard to see. There was a park I was familiar with coming up soon. I put on my hazard lights and slowed down. I wanted to say so many things to my girl-friend, but I was afraid anything I said might make it worse.

We reached the park and I came to a complete stop. I said nothing. She was looking out of her side window. Putting my hand on her chin and pulling her face toward me, I whispered how I felt.

"If I've done anything to upset you, I'm sorry."

"No, Perry. It's not you. It's just sometimes things don't work out perfectly. My best friend trying to come on to you is a little much. A lot of girls give me drama. I know they're jealous and stuff. So what, I can run really fast? I'm breaking a few records. Yeah, my grades are great. I study hard. It's not some rocket scientist stuff, but I am a smart girl. People don't even know you and there's like rumbling around my school that we're dating and now I'm hated ten times more than I was before. It's like crazy. I'm just sick of it."

"You're preaching to the choir, girl. I get mess like that all the time. Most of the time I don't know what people's beef with me is, you know?"

"Yeah, I know. But the way they look at you lets you know they got issues," she said.

"Exactly. But you gotta do what I do."

"What? Tell me because this hurts. I mean, this time it was my best friend."

"You just got to let it go, shake it off and realize that there are some things that you just can't control. That serenity prayer is for real."

"How does it go again?" she asked, as I looked into her eyes.

Her vulnerability made me see her in such an awesome light. I wanted to hold her tight and let her know it was okay. She was too sweet to be dealing with unhappy people.

"God grant me the serenity to accept the things that I cannot change, the courage to change the things that I can, and the wisdom to know the difference."

"Yes. Yes. That's how it goes," she said, reaching over and gently squeezing my jaw. "I can't control Ellis's actions or those of my dumb brother. I mean, he doesn't even really like her, but because he thought you were coming on to her, he was ticked. That is so stupid."

"It's other people's insecurities. We can't let them come between us. As long as we stay true to this, what we're building, it'll be built solid like brick, and won't nobody be able to huff it down."

"Ahh, Perry," she said as she gently stroked my face with the back of her hand and dangled her index finger under my chin for a minute.

Then she worked her finger to the corner of my lip and I kissed it until I was actually caught up sucking it. When she pulled her finger away, her lips were practically touching mine. I had no problem putting my hands behind her head as I pulled her toward me. The kiss of passion that we shared was explosive, more dynamic than the lightning around us.

"Perry, I really care for you," she said as she eased away from me.

"I care for you too," I said as I tried to find my way back to those luscious lips. But she stopped me.

"No, I really care about you. The feeling is so strong I don't trust myself around you. And right now in your arms— oh my gosh, what am I saying?"

All of a sudden she opened the door and jumped out. Quickly I popped the trunk of my car and searched through my things in the back and got out my big, black umbrella. I ran over to Savoy and covered her.

"It's not safe out here," I said. "Come back in the car with me."

She said, "You don't understand. It's safer out here in the thunder and lightning than back in the car with you, making all the rumble. You know what I'm saying?"

"We can do this."

She got on her tiptoes and kissed me again. As certain as I was at first that we would be okay and not cross the line and further displease God, after that next kiss out there in the rain, the umbrella was suddenly gone and so was my conviction. Then out of nowhere, lightning hit the ground just feet away from us, and it shocked both of us back into some kind of spiritual reality.

"We can't do this," I said. "I care about you too, Savoy, and not just because I'm trying to get a piece."

"I hear girls talking at school. Ellis in particular. Telling me if I don't give it up to you soon that I will lose you. I know we just started dating, but I don't think I will feel any closer to you a year from now than I do right now. A big part of me wants to. I don't want any barriers between us."

"I know Savoy, but people can't pressure you into having sex with me. Man, that's just not what I want from you. I mean, I do want that from you, but I want it because you want to give it to me and when you want to give it to me, and when we both think it's right. They don't know what we are trying to build. And in reality, we really don't know each other that well. I mean, yeah, you're the coolest girl I've ever met. Real and all that. I know you won't ever get any more beautiful than you are to me right now, but man, I wouldn't be able to live with myself if I let you give it up when you really weren't sure."

I led Savoy back to the car and when we got in I scrambled around in the back seat searching for a towel. I found it and gave it to her, then got my sweatshirt and wiped my face.

"I'm a mess. My mascara is running all down my face."

"I meant it outside when I said you were gorgeous."

"So what are we supposed to do with this?" she asked. "This attraction that we feel so strong. Huh?"

"Well, we go to different schools and there's going to be guys, what, hitting on my girl."

"What, I know, there's going to be girls throwing themselves at you, and it's clear your ex is one of them."

We continued to share our hearts with each other. We were so open that I loved the communication we had going. All of a sudden, I felt the desire to pray. God knew I was in trouble and that I was trying to do the right thing. The spirit inside of me was saying: *Lead boy. Lead. Lead my way and not your way. Don't let the loins go first. Pray.* I looked over at Savoy and spoke what the spirit said to me.

"Can we pray?"

"Yeah, that's a great idea," she said, smiling.

I took her hand and began.

"Father, thank you for sending me a girl like Savoy. Not only is she so adorable on the outside, but she cares about You, and I see Your spirit shining in her on the inside. But we ain't right, Lord. Some things are rising up in this car and it isn't just steam."

Savoy chuckled a little.

"We truly need your help. We want to please You. We want

to try to be abstinent and we know that's not the popular choice. Help us. Make the choice for us. Help us not to be pressured to do anything less than Your will. In Jesus' name we pray."

"Amen," we said together.

"So you really saw Ellis trying to come on to me?" I asked, very curious.

"Yeah. Your mom saw it too. She pulled me around the corner and we checked out my friend's actions. Or, shall I say, we checked out her sly, trifling ways. Your mom was real cool. She told me you wouldn't let me down, and she was right."

"I didn't want to hurt you," I said, turning away.

"Perry Skky Jr., look at me." I looked directly into her eyes. "We're going to be okay. God's got us."

I felt good as I listened to those words and the way she said them. I knew we were building something special, and I was excited. At that moment, I knew that I was fully committing my heart.

~ 7 ~

Desiring a Fix

"Perry, I love you. I need you," Tori said, as she caught me off guard and kissed me as I sat in the stands at the basketball game.

Instinctively, I kissed her back. But where was this coming from? I mean, it did feel good, but for goodness sakes, I was at a basketball game. My boy Damarius had led Lucy Laney to the playoffs. To get away from my current situation with Tori, I pulled away and went to an isolated restroom.

Before I knew it the lights were out, and somebody locked the door. That somebody was Tori, and she was all over me. The weird thing was that I was all over her as well. I ain't gon' lie. And those painted-on jeans she wore made it easier for me to grip her behind.

"See, Perry. You haven't forgotten about me. I'm gon' make you feel good."

When she went probing around to find my zipper, I said, "Wait, wait. Hold up, girl."

I just didn't understand why life had to be so complicated all the time. I was just with my girl. Shucks! With all the fondling going on with Tori I couldn't even remember my girlfriend's name. Savoy, yeah. I was just with Savoy. Things with Savoy were perfect.

Well, they weren't perfect at first, of course. But Valentine's night was a bit special. And here it was not even a full week later and my lips were locking with my ex. The sad part was, a part of me didn't wanna stop. And I knew that was crazy.

So I said, "Look, Tori. This is crazy. You know we can't do this."

"You keep saying we can't do this, but I know you want me just as much."

When we kissed again, I finally realized why she was so aggressive. "Tori, you've been drinking!"

"Ciara and I just had a little wine cooler. But I feel good. I feel like I wanna make you feel even better."

Completely upset, I finally found the light switch, flipped it on, and noticed her sweater was unbuttoned. "Listen. Fix yourself. You're too good for this."

"Too good for what, Perry? To want to be with the guy I love? Because I wanted to stay so pure and so perfect, I pushed you away. Now you're with a new girl, and I know y'all getting it on. She hasn't invested in you as much as I have. I love you. And I want you back."

"You are drunk," I told her.

"So what? You think I don't know what I'm saying? Just because I might need a little buzz to help me relax, I'm not gonna let you drive me away. I won't! You love me, Perry. You do!"

I didn't mean to push her to tears, but that's exactly what happened. My girl just started bawling all in front of me. Wait, what was I saying? Tori wasn't my girl anymore. I was completely tripping.

"I got to get back to the game. You need to stop this, girl," I said as I unlocked the bathroom door to exit.

But she charged up against the door and pushed it shut. Then she flung herself backwards and slightly banged her head on the door. The tears came faster this time around. I went over to the sink and wet a paper towel. I was trying to comfort her and trying to let her know that I still cared about her, but not in the way that she wanted it to be.

Yeah, sure. Any guy would've taken what she was giving away and had his way with her, no feelings attached. A part of me felt that same way. But I wasn't just some guy with no feelings; no concern over what was right or wrong. Though I wanted to take care of my needs badly and Tori knew what buttons to push, there was just something else making me accountable for this wake-up call.

I realized that it was the Holy Spirit, working deep inside of me. I wasn't a punk. I wasn't scared to let her go down on me. And I doggone sure wasn't gay. But I was okay with the fact that this wasn't God's will. Though it really bothered me to see her so broken again, I knew it bothered me more that I was contemplating breaking my vow with God just to please my flesh.

Handing her a paper towel I said, "Look. I really do care about you."

"It's the other girl, right? She's got something to do with it."

"If I was dating you, you wouldn't want me to step out on you. I never cheated on you. Yeah, I remember Amandi was coming on strong to me and all that one time, and I broke it off. Come on, Tori. I wish you could see yourself as I see you. Well, at least the Tori I used to know."

"How have I changed, Perry? Why don't you love me anymore? You didn't use to care what I wanted, only about what God wanted."

"You aren't trying to give up like Ciara and Briana are. Your girls are a little hot and my boys don't deserve them either, but you just have higher standards. As I much as I was trying to get in your panties, you wasn't having that."

I didn't mean to get graphic with it, but I had to be real. She was asking me how and why she changed in my eyes. And the truth is she was too pitiful for me to want to be with.

Seeing her mouth droop, I said, "Don't look at me that way, I'm only being honest."

"Go ahead."

"You act like if I'm not in your world, you're going to break in two. If that's how you want to carry yourself then you do that. But really you're not feeling bad because you need me."

"But I do need you. I can't sleep, still thinking about what we had. Every time my phone rings I'm hoping that it's you. I drank a little something and followed you to the teachers' restroom so I could take advantage of you. I don't feel good right now. I guess I just thought you would want me. I don't know, Perry."

"Tori, you gotta go back to what's important to you. You gotta take all your problems to God. I'm just a guy who has many faults but God won't fail you, you know? Give him a try."

She couldn't say anything so she nodded her head. She wiped her face and she motioned for me to head on out. I gave her a thumbs up and when she gave me that sign back, I felt like I had to give her space. Allow her a moment to get back into a tight relationship with the only one that could please her completely.

As I shut the door and prayed for her, I hoped she would get what she needed. And thanking the Lord that he allowed me to make the right call, I prayed, "*And you better be thankful you came when you did 'cause I was about to get my groove on*!"

"Man, I can't believe you talked us into spending our Sunday on the road with you," Damarius joked, as he and Cole rode with me to Conyers.

I wasn't excited either to make a two-hour drive to see my grandmother. But it had been a while since I'd had one of her good meals or even seen her for that matter. She had been down for Thanksgiving and every time I talked to her she asked me when I was coming to visit. Her regular maintenance guy that cuts her lawn was sick and instead of asking one of her friends from church to help her, she talked my dad into making me come.

And I guess I couldn't complain. I didn't even really know my mom's parents, who were estranged from her. So my father's folks were the only ones I knew, and since my dad's father died over a year ago, I felt really sad about my grandmother being alone.

So I messed with my boys and said, "Oh, come on now. I know y'all ready to get your grub on."

"Oh, I ain't complaining," Cole said from the passenger side. "Grandma be hooking us up. I'm too ready for some of that good old fried chicken, mashed potatoes, ham, chitlins, collard greens, and corn on the cob. She be setting it off. I'm gonna get out the car, get ready to cut the grass, and get ready to chow down! We can put Damarius out right now and I'll take his share."

"So, you gon' do me like that?" Damarius said as he undid his seatbelt and popped Cole on the head.

"All right, children. Settle down," I said to my two friends. "For real though. Grandma is weird sometimes."

"I know, man. She was trying to come on to me one time," Damarius teased.

"That's what I'm saying. I don't know if she gonna be standoffish or overly friendly."

Damarius asked, "She ain't got that Allminers does she, boy?"

"You so dumb. It's all *timers*. Ain't that right, Perry?" Cole said.

I could only laugh at the two of them. "It's Alzheimer's."

Before we knew it, we were pulling up to my grandmother's place. And though it was March and the grass hadn't started growing yet, hers was tall and off the chain with weeds and all kinds of bushes we needed to cut down.

"'Bout time you boys got here. Perry, you didn't get lost, did you?" my grandmother said as she greeted us at the front door.

"Hey to you too, Grandma," I said, as my boys started to laugh.

It wasn't long before she put us to work. An hour and thirty minutes later, I was thirsty. I asked my boys if they wanted something, but they both passed on the water and said they were waiting on the tea. When I came inside to quench my thirst, I was surprised to see her slumped over like she was hurting badly. "Grandma, what's wrong?"

"Aww, baby. I just need to take some more medicine. Sorry I've been acting crabby, but I ain't been feeling too good."

"Daddy didn't tell me you were sick," I said, rubbing her back.

She flung my hand off her. "Oh, boy. Go on back out there. Don't you be worrying about an old woman."

"Grandma, you are not an old woman." Then she fell onto her couch. "Grandma, something serious is going on with you. Tell me. What's wrong?"

"Boy, didn't I tell you I'd be okay? Now you ain't never around here. You remind me of your granddaddy. Coming in here trying to control somebody. I can take care of myself."

"Just worried about you, Grandma. That's all," I said, chuckling, as she got onto me.

That's when I knew she was okay, so I went back outside. I wasn't out there ten minutes before Damarius said he wanted something to drink.

"Uh-uh! I asked you did you want a drink. You better go in

there yourself and get something. We 'bout to eat in five minutes, can't you wait? Grandma already got the food on the table."

"No, I can't wait! I'm thirsty. You couldn't wait."

"Just go ahead then."

There was no need for me to fuss with my friend. Cole and I tried to finish the work. All of a sudden Damarius rushed back outside.

"P, you won't believe this." Damarius was waving frantically for me to stop cutting.

"What? What's going on with you? You see I got this big lawnmower in my hand. You trying to make me cut my foot?"

"Your grandma's smoking a joint."

"Yeah, right, boy. You the one on crack. That ain't right for you to talk about folks' grandma," Cole said. "Particularly right before we eat."

"Does it look like I'm laughing or joking, man?" He turned off the lawnmower for me. "Perry, I'm serious. You need to go check on her."

I went in the house after telling my two friends to stay outside. I mean, it's not like I believed Damarius. I don't know. I just had to check it out. The bathroom door was open, and when I walked in, I saw my grandmother sitting on the toilet stool with a rolled up Zig-Zag in her hand.

"Grandma! What are you doing?" She tried to place it down by her side. "You can't hide anything. I've already seen what you were doing. What is going on? Let me call my dad right now."

"All right, boy. You just get back in here. I raised your daddy and spanked his tail. And doggone it, I can spank yours too. Now, get back in here and let me explain. I was feeling too good to have to deal with this foolishness."

"Foolishness? Grandma, you were smoking an illegal substance. What are you doing?"

After she put the joint down, I was so surprised at what she told me next. My heart stopped.

"Perry, I got lung cancer. I used to smoke back in the day and I guess it caught up with me. Your granddad told me to quit. And this is a little medicine my friend Miss Mae told me about. Now nobody needs to know about this. You hear me?" she said, as she got in my face.

No wonder she had so many mood swings. No wonder she was so emotional. I was afraid to ask her how sick she was, but when she told me that smoking pot made her feel better I told her that I'd act like I never saw a thing.

I explained it to my boys as we ate dinner. And when we drove home we vowed to keep this between us. As much as I hadn't wanted to make the drive up there, I was glad that I did go and found out what was really going on in Conyers. I prayed that what she was doing was good for her. I kept quiet. Who was I to get in the way?

The next weekend I had successfully put the incident with my grandmother out of my mind. The old woman was past grown. She told me herself she raised my dad and she assured me that she didn't need to be parented. She knew what she was doing.

When I came from working out I was surprised to see my sister's car in the driveway. Though I hadn't admitted it to Payton, I had missed her a lot around here. When I passed by her room, I stopped in my tracks. Though the door was shut I heard crying from the other side.

Without knocking I opened the door. "What's up, Pay? Why you sad?" I said to her with my arms folded, ready for an explanation so I could fix her problem.

"Perry, I'm all right. I just need some time to myself. Can you give me that, please?"

I didn't wanna tell her no. I figured she knew my answer was negative when I didn't move.

"Sis, you're crying. I'm not just gonna leave you like this."

I hated to say it but she was a girl and there could be a lot of things wrong with her. That time of the month. Some girl at school didn't like her. Whatever it was I knew it didn't have anything to do with her boyfriend Tad. She and her boyfriend were so tight. He was a good Christian guy. He had given his word that he wouldn't change on my sister. He loved her too much to break her heart.

When she saw I was still waiting on an answer she stood in front of me saying, "It's Tad."

I was blown away. That was the last thing I was expecting her to say. What had he done? The boy was practically perfect. I guess she sensed from my bewildered look that I couldn't believe he was causing the problem between them. It had to be her.

"Yes, it's me," she said.

"I thought so," I responded. "Why you tripping now?"

"Perry, am I attractive?"

"What?" I questioned, knowing she was freaking out.

"I mean, I know I'm your sister but let's just say I wasn't your sister. Would you think I was cute, the bomb?"

"No, not right now. You look a hot mess," I joked, trying to lighten the mood.

"I'm serious," she said as she jabbed me in the shoulder, pushing me a few feet back I might add. My sister had strength. "Perry, seriously, what do you think? Is your sister a dime or what?"

"Man, that's a really silly question, considering I still got folks asking 'bout you. Dakari would take you back any minute even though you wouldn't give him the time of day. Why do you think Tad isn't interested in you?"

"I shouldn't be talking 'bout this to my little brother."

"I'm not your little brother, girl. I'm a senior in high school and about to be in the big world like you. Don't get it twisted."

"And you're going to Georgia Tech. I shouldn't be talking to you anyway, you traitor."

"Ain't nothing wrong with having a little friendly state competition in the house. Even though you're a cheerleader at Georgia I know you're going to be cheering your brother on when I take the field."

"You know it," she said, as she gave me a wink. "But I'm a dawg at heart."

"Whatever," I told her. "So, you gon' try me or what? We've been through a lot, Payton. If I trust you with what I say then same here."

"You have grown up."

"Girl, please. I remember how devastated you were the first day of your senior year over Dakari leaving you for another girl. Who helped you out and made you smile? Huh?"

"You're so silly, boy. But you're right. And at the time you were a sophomore trying to fight a senior."

"I scared his butt too."

"I think you were a nerd then, Perry. And that stunt made your status go way up. You have me to thank."

Cutting up with Payton was cool. We hadn't had much time to connect, with her away and all. I just hoped she'd trust me talk about what had her in tears earlier.

"Yeah, right. So what's up with you and Tad?"

"Okay, here it goes. You should understand because you're also an angel?"

"No, I'm not an angel."

"But you love God and try to do the right thing, right?"

"Yeah," I told her. "What is it?"

"My boyfriend is the finest thing on campus."

"Okay, that's way too much info. Maybe you need to talk to Mom about this," I said, as I was turning and walking away.

"Boy, sit down!" she said as she pushed me. "I really asked myself am I gonna go to hell if I have sex before I'm married. God'll forgive me, right? And maybe it's not so wrong because I really love Tad. Maybe I should consider how we feel about each other."

"Consider what, girl? Y'all ain't married."

"Don't act like you don't know what I'm talking about, Mr. Girls Trying To Give It Up Everywhere You Turn! And you just said yourself you weren't an angel."

"All right. Dang!"

"So how are you and Savoy doing? Good?"

"Yeah, Tad's cousin is straight. My ex ain't doing too bad either." My sister looked at me as if I had crossed some line. The line she was just thinking about crossing herself. "We're cool if that's what you wanna call it. Though I still like Tori a lot."

"Of course Savoy is adorable. And it's not like we're going through the same thing because you don't even know who you love. I made a clear decision between Dakari and Tad. I dated Dakari in high school and when he cheated on me, I never gave him another chance. Yeah, me and Dakari stayed cool afterward but I still chose Tad. Now we have a strong bond. Girls go up to him all the time and we overcome that. And now I want him to want me physically as well as emotionally, you know."

"Sis, I got it, okay."

"Is that so wrong? I mean, I look at him and I just want to tear off his clothes."

"Trust me. I don't know what you're talking about."

"Perry, quit being silly. I'm sure you want to get with one of those girls."

I wasn't gonna lie. She already knew the truth, being the big sister she was. And I knew where she was coming from. It was hard for me, too.

"What are we going to do? We want it so bad but God says that it's something we can't have. And that has caused a lot of problems with me and Tad. Tad says that if I can't drop the subject and really honor the fact that he's trying to live his life then he's gonna break up with me. And I can't believe he'd actually do that. I mean, I'm glad that he loves God more than he loves me but he's telling me he would choose God over me. But I am afraid I can't control this urge."

"How 'bout we just pray? We both need it. But I know when I call on God, sis, He helps me out of stuff. And that passion I feel just goes away. God can help us control those feelings so that we don't give in to our flesh. I think it's that time."

"You really think praying will help? I don't wanna lose my boyfriend. I don't know, Perry."

"Sis, you just gotta trust Him. You gotta know that the Holy Spirit inside of you is ready to work. But if you don't activate it, if you don't ask Him to help you conquer all the tough stuff you're feeling then you're in a battle with yourself. It's actually like you're in the ring with Satan. That's no match."

"I never thought of it like that."

"Yeah, you know. Once you tell the Holy Spirit to take it, He fights your battles. You think Satan wanna go against that?"

My sister and I spent the next few minutes praying. It was weird 'cause Payton had led me most of the way through my Christian walk and now here I was helping her through a tough time. It's funny how the tables turn. God was really holding me up and I loved that.

I understood where she was and how hard it was to fight off your own urges. But I truly believed once you gave all that to God, He'd be the one we longed for. On God, we'd be desiring a fix.

~ 8 ~

Seeing Someone Die

"So I see you wanna live, huh?" the infamous Jaboe said as he sat beside me on the bleachers at another big game.

I was ready to see Damarius lead us to success into the second round of the playoffs. And all of a sudden, I got a little nervous. I was surrounded by thugs. It was like Jaboe couldn't be alone. He had to carry his intimidation crew with him. I didn't want him to know, but the fear factor was working on me.

"What's up, Perry? You don't hear me talking to you? You too good to talk to me now?" he taunted.

"Man, I'm just getting ready for the game, that's all."

"I'm here to watch the game too. I'm here trying to give you props and you ignoring me. I thought you was acting right, telling our boy to stay in the game with me. But if you wanna treat me like I got the plague, man, people get killed for less. You better watch your back."

When I finally stood up to his game, I said, "So, you threatening me?"

"Oh, now he speaks!" he said sarcastically.

"Nah. Just making you aware that's all. I told you at the be-ginning of the year that your thing was your thing, Jaboe. I honored that. So I don't think we have no business to talk about, do we?"

We locked eyes for a minute. He didn't flinch and I didn't move either. That is until I heard Cole say, "J man, can I have my seat back?"

"Come on, y'all. Let's get outta here," Jaboe said to his homies, without saying another word to me or Cole.

Cole handed me a large Sprite and nachos from the concession stand. I knew he wanted to ask me something but I didn't wanna go there.

"Aww, come on, Perry," Cole said as he stomped his large foot, jarring the people around us.

"Come on what, man? Calm down. I don't know what you're talking 'bout."

"No, you don't know what you're getting into. Tell me you ain't doing drugs with that fool?"

"Boy! You know better than that," I told my friend.

"Know exactly what? All them surrounding you like that I thought I was gonna have to spill the soda in their face. Get physical and bust somebody," my big buddy said.

Cole was fearless on the football field, a defensive end that could throw any offensive lineman, running back, tight end, or quarterback all over the place. I had no doubt that he probably could make a dent in Jaboe's game. But thuggin' wasn't his nature off the field. And I certainly wouldn't want him to lose his integrity because of me.

So I quickly said, "Look. He was just asking me about Damarius."

"Damarius? I thought that boy stopped doing stuff with him."

"That's my partner."

"That's my partner too. If one of us get hurt, all of us get hurt."

"All right. I'm just saying that's all he wanted."

Thankfully, Damarius led our basketball team onto the court. Folks around us started cheering and it got too loud for me to hear Cole's response.

"Man, let's just watch the game."

"Fine!" Cole yelled, a little agitated at me. "I'm just glad you ain't doing it."

"Believe me, I ain't messing with him one bit."

"I knew you were too smart for that."

At halftime, we were down by fifteen points. Damarius was having a horrible game. And when I looked over at the bench, he and the coach were going at it. I didn't think that he was going to be able to get back on track. But he went back on the court and I yelled anyway for my friend to step it up.

"Come on D! You can win this, man!"

"Yeah, boy!" Cole screamed, helping me egg him on. "Quit playing around and show them your real game."

Though the place was packed, he found us. He looked into the stands, and gave us a thumbs up.

"It's on now, y'all," Cole said into the crowd. "Our boy's about to play."

He had the ball in his hand. He twirled it around to the left side, changed hands, and evaded an opponent on the right. Went to the three-point line, shot it, and missed.

"Dang it!" I said. "That's all right, partner. That's all right."

I tried to stay positive for the moment 'cause everybody has a bad game every now and then. But this was an important game. Damarius couldn't afford to lose so pitifully. Suddenly, he fouled a guy. Then Coach sat him out for a few minutes. When he got back in the game, he missed his next three shots.

"What's really up with D, man? Looks like he's really throwing the game now," Cole said.

And then it dawned on me. Did Jaboe force my friend to

lose so he could make some money? Stranger things had happened. I was so pissed. I knew Damarius was a hothead but he knew how to keep it together more than he was displaying at this important time in his life.

He was excited about this particular game, ready to keep winning so that he could get a basketball scholarship. He was pulling up his grades and for him to play so poorly, I knew this was killing him.

"Man, something ain't right with the boy," Cole said, pointing to our friend. "He makes free throw shots in his sleep and I don't think he's made one since he's been out there."

Finally, Coach benched him for good. We were now down twenty-five points and the crowd booed him as he went to his seat. He took a towel and placed it over his head and leaned over, like he didn't wanna see anyone. Like he didn't wanna be there. As the clock wound down, we knew there was no way that our team could rev up. We lost. At the end of the game, even his teammates seemed to be terribly disappointed in Damarius.

Jaboe came up to me and sarcastically said, "Heartbreaking game, wasn't it?

That sealed it for me. Some way, somehow he had gotten to Damarius and told him how to perform. So concerned about his money that he didn't give a care about my boy's future. If I had a brick, I swear I would've smashed his face in. Such an arrogant loser, and yet I was crippled by his ways.

Jaboe announced with excitement, "But don't sweat it, people. Don't fret. Come out to the parking lot 'cause Jaboe's throwing a jam!"

I went over to Damarius before he headed into the locker room and he said, "Man. I just couldn't help it. I had to and I feel so low right now."

He walked away into the locker room. I watched him leave, and realized that messing with the wrong people is suicide.

He basically threw a big part of his life away, and even though he knew it wasn't worth it, he knew he hadn't had a choice. The whole ordeal was sad.

"So, what? We staying?" Cole said to me, as we tried to make our way out of the crowded gym.

"No, man. I'm going home. I was just trying to talk to Damarius for a second and see if he wanted to grab something to eat or whatever, but I ain't staying around for no parking lot party. The cops will be here before that thing even begins."

"All right. Well, let me just talk to my girl. She's over there with Ciara and Tori. You can say something to Tori too. Just because you don't want to be with the old girl no more, don't mean you can't be her friend."

I rolled my eyes as I followed Cole over to the girls. I wanted to talk to Ciara anyway. She could help make Damarius feel better. But I couldn't even get with her because she was chasing down a bottle of wine. So I went over to Tori.

"What's your girl doing?"

"We're just having a little fun that's all. Some of us are really hurting and we don't need goody-two-shoes Perry Skky Jr. telling us all what sinners we are."

"Tori, you been drinking at this game too?" I said as I noticed my ex's breath reeking of alcohol.

"You better go talk to your boy, Perry!" Ciara turned around and said real loud.

"Well I need you to do that for me," I yelled back.

"Yeah, right. I'm sure he'll take it out on me that he played like crap."

"Oh, come on Ciara. You need to cut him a break now."

"Cut him a break? We're not going to the state championship because of him," Ciara mouthed off.

Damarius came from around the cars with Jaboe and his

boys. He had a pipe in his hand and I knew he'd been smoking weed. Then he picked up his swagger pace and headed over to Ciara. I tried to get between them but he pushed me away.

"Man, get back!"

"Yeah, move, Perry. Let him come at me. His weak play tells me he ain't about nothing," Ciara said.

"Oh, so you gon' talk about my game like that? Calling me out in front of these people and stuff?" he yelled before he got over to her.

I lunged at him again and Jaboe stepped in my way. So I eased back. When Damarius got over to his girl, he grabbed her by the arm.

"Get your hands off of me! Stop D! I love you!" Ciara cried out.

But Damarius didn't stop. He slapped her. I knew weed made sane people do crazy things, but witnessing him trip first-hand was more than I could take. Ciara screamed.

Almost instantly, Cole stepped in and took Damarius and Ciara off somewhere. I stood there with a bunch of classmates I didn't know well, plus Tori, Briana, Jaboe and his same intimidating crew.

"Don't even think about moving, boy," Jaboe said to me when our eyes met again. "He's just handling his business with his girl. She's supposed to always have his back."

I said, "My friend doesn't hit on a woman."

"My friend does," he replied.

Tori ran up to me crying. "You could've done something, Perry. He's hitting her!"

"You just told me to stay out of it and now you want me to do something?" I was still upset with her for drinking.

Damarius came back over to the crowd. "See, that's why I'm through with your tired tail. You think I'm so pathetic and a loser? Well, fine. You can't satisfy me anyway. We're through."

"No, no, no. Don't break up with me!" Ciara ran up behind him as Cole struggled to keep up.

Here he was hitting her and calling her worthless and she still wanted to be with him. Oh, heck no. They needed a break from each other. They weren't in their right minds. As I walked toward her, Jaboe stepped into my path a third time.

I said, "Hey, you want me to take care of this? D can't hustle for you in the streets if he's in jail."

"See, now you're starting to understand my game." He backed out of my way.

I went over to Damarius and Ciara. They continued to scream at each other. I tugged my boy away from her.

Hoping to get through to him, I said, "Come on, Damarius. Let's cool down."

"Man, leave me alone." Damarius jerked his arm away.

"Boy let's go cool down, before you say something you'll regret."

Ciara rushed up to him, dropped to her knees and grabbed him at the ankles, pleading for him to stay her boyfriend. The whole scene was ridiculous.

Damarius yelled, "You need to get away from me right now, Ciara."

He started shaking his leg to get her off. But when that tactic didn't work, the boy I thought I knew went beyond insane. He kicked her in the face.

Ciara scrambled back and yelled, "Forget you, Damarius!"

He charged back at her and I got in the way. "Man, stop acting crazy."

"Oh, so you calling me crazy now too?"

"Man, just settle down," I responded, trying not to anger him more.

"Come on, Perry. I'm sick of you thinking you're God's gift to the world. Like you're so great in football you can do no wrong!"

I didn't have to respond to his nonsense. I knew my buddy was higher than an airplane thirty thousand miles in the air. I wanted to tell him so bad to leave Jaboe alone but I didn't. I knew I couldn't make that move or I would risk losing too much if that video tape ever got out.

"I'm so sick of you, man," Damarius said to me. "You act like you're the only one who hears God."

"What are you talking about? Where'd that come from? But he is really who you need right now," I said to him. "I know Cole agrees with me."

"You mean your little hand puppet?" I hadn't realized that Cole was standing behind me until Damarius looked over my shoulder. "Yeah, I'm talking about you, man. Every time I wanna do something, it's 'Let me check with Perry,'" Damarius said, mocking him. "Can't you think for your doggone self? What you gonna do when you're at USC and your boy ain't there?"

"I won't get high and drunk and throw my life away, that's for sure," Cole snapped.

Damarius ran toward him but I was standing right there. I couldn't allow my two best friends to fight and make matters worse.

"This is not going down like this," I said.

"Ain't nobody thinking 'bout you." Damarius drew his arm back.

"Tori, let me go. Let me go!" Ciara shouted. "I just wanna talk to him. He can't break up with me. I don't wanna end up like you and Perry. We've been living our lives for these guys for the past two years and you think just because he says some dumb stuff that I'm gonna give that up? I will do whatever I can to keep him. I refuse to end up like you, Tori. I don't want to hurt your feelings and I know I've been drinking, but you cry every night over Perry. You be bugging me to hang out with you and I neglect my own boyfriend because of you. It's sad and I don't want to be like that. I don't."

I couldn't believe what I was hearing. Seemed Tori had been going through a lot since we broke up. And Ciara was making it clear that I broke a part of Tori's spirit. I turned around and looked over at the both of them. As Ciara went walking over to Damarius, Tori stood there with tears streaming down her face.

Cole stopped Ciara and said, "Y'all two need to just chill out for a minute. You know he loves you, girl."

"I love you, baby," Ciara yelled to Damarius. "You know I do."

Damarius swung his hand in the air. "Whatever."

"That's right, man. Let her know who's boss. Make her beg to get back with you," Jaboe said.

Ciara broke down crying again and Tori and Briana comforted her. When I heard a car engine rev up very loudly, I turned and saw Ciara in the driver's seat. Tori and Briana were with her, trying to get her out of the car. All three of them had been drinking too heavily to drive.

"Cole, stop them!" I called out.

Maybe I could fix this. Maybe I could get it back where it used to be when all of us were together.

"Ciara think she can drive?" Damarius came to me and said with concern. "She better go straight home 'cause she know better than to drink and drive. She just got her license."

I didn't have a good feeling about this at all.

It was like time stood still for a moment as I thought about all the happy times among the six of us. We went to the movies together, Six Flags, and we had even snuck off to the beach last summer. In a way I felt partly responsible for the current mess. My breakup with Tori wasn't just a breakup between us, but clearly I could now see it was a breakup of our group. And it affected her much more deeply than I imagined.

She was severely depressed because even her friends thought her losing me made her nothing. And that was so wrong. All I wanted to do was go hug her and let her know that she had it going on way before I entered the picture. And she could go do her thing and be strong again.

I still cared for her and a part of me still loved her. But could I help her? I watched as Cole gave up on trying to get Ciara out of the car. As he stepped back, Tori and Briana climbed inside.

Damarius started to get his senses back. "I'm sorry, Perry. I hit her. I hit you. I just lost my head, man. I don't know."

"Come on man," Jaboe shouted from a few feet away. "I got plenty of other girls that wanna get with you."

"Man, I'm straight. I gotta go get my girl and set things right."

"That's cool, dog. But we got more work to do, so don't take too long to find me."

"I'll hook up with you later, promise," Damarius whispered in his ear. "I took care of the game for you, so just let me do something for me."

I hated hearing my friend plead for some space from Jaboe. He practically admitted that he threw the game for him.

"I can't believe you're not going to say anything to him," Cole said to me. "He shouldn't be asking for approval from a drug dealer. You used to care, Perry. Say something."

"Look, right now do you see their car going full speed towards that main street?" I said, frantically pointing at the ride the girls were in. "Your girl is in that car. Let's go get them before they do something stupid."

"Yeah. Briana got mad at me cause I told her I couldn't hang out with her because I was hanging out with you."

"Did you know the three of them were drinking like that?" I asked.

"Yeah, I knew it made her a little loose and little free. She's been doing some really kinky stuff lately," Cole said smiling. "I like it when she gets a little buzz."

"That car better slow down! There's an eighteen-wheeler!" I heard some girl yell out from the crowd.

"Ciara, stop!" Damarius shouted as he saw the potential danger.

Ciara sped out of the school parking lot just as a truck approached going pretty fast. There was no way the driver would be able to stop. And he shouldn't have to because he had the right of way. Everyone around me started running toward the street.

I stood frozen as the eighteen-wheeler slammed into the front end of the girls' car, sending it spinning a ways before it tumbled over. I was horrified by the sight.

"Oh my gosh! Who was in there?" someone yelled from behind us.

Quickly, Cole and Damarius and I hopped in my car and sped over to the wreck. I knew the girls had to be okay. My mind could comprehend nothing else.

"Someone call nine-one-one!" I shouted as we got out of the car.

"You guys need to stay back," some boy said to the three of us.

But Cole, Damarius, and myself were hearing no such thing. They were in there. They had to be okay.

"We gotta get the car back upright," I said.

"Maybe we shouldn't mess with it, man. That might make stuff worse," Cole suggested to me.

I was just pacing back and forth by the wreck. "Tori! Can

you hear me? Briana? Ciara? Y'all? Say something." No one responded.

After what felt like hours, we heard sirens coming toward us.

"Does anybody know what happened here?" the police officer asked as the ambulance and fire truck attended to the car and truck.

Damarius rushed up to the officer and Cole held him back.

I went over and said, "Sir, the car pulled out into the path of the eighteen-wheeler."

"There was a big game here tonight. Did you know the people in the car, young man?" the officer asked.

"Yes, sir. That's my girlfriend and her two friends."

Nothing mattered at that moment to me. Not football. Not college. Not even Savoy. I just wanted Tori to be okay and I would give anything for that to happen. When the rescuers got Briana out of the backseat, people cheered when they saw that she was okay. Cole ran over to her side even though the emergency workers told him to get back. There was blood all over her pants. Her leg appeared broken and was covered with shattered glass.

"She's all right, y'all!" Cole shouted, thrilled she was alive.

A paramedic said, "I'm sorry, sir, but you can't ride with us to the hospital. You can follow."

Briana squealed, "Please, let him come. I'm scared."

"Ma'am, he'll see you at the hospital."

"How's Tori and Ciara?" she asked.

Cole held his head down and said, "We don't know right now. They're still working to get them out the car."

"Tori! Ciara!" Briana called out.

This was not a cool feeling at all. I was so shaken up that I couldn't keep still. The truck driver was unconscious. And I prayed that he'd be okay. It wasn't his fault and I'm sure the officer knew that. As I prayed for him, I prayed for Tori too. A smile came across my face when I heard her call out for me. She had a big cut across her forehead.

"Oh, my gosh, Perry. I was so scared," she said when they pulled her from the wreckage.

"*You* were scared?" I held her hand when they put her on the gurney. "Girl, I was scared to see that truck hit you guys."

Tori asked, "Where's Briana? Where's Ciara?"

"Briana's fine. I think you're gonna ride with her in the ambulance."

"I don't need to go to the hospital. I need to make sure Ciara is okay."

"No, you need to go and get checked out," I told her.

Another ambulance and another fire truck arrived on the scene. People were screaming and Damarius was pacing back and forth fussing at every worker to hurry and get Ciara out of the car.

"This car is gon' blow," a firefighter yelled out.

"Oh, my gosh! Ciara's in that car," Tori said.

"Sweetie, you gotta calm down," I said to her before seeing her into the ambulance and assuring her that I'd be there shortly.

"Perry, you gotta call my parents and tell them what happened. Then you gotta come to the hosptial. Please come."

"Don't worry. I'll call your folks and I'll come. I promise. You have to let these people get a look at that head, okay. It's not gon' help with you freaking out and stuff."

She lay back and allowed the paramedics to work on her. How do you tell anyone's parents that their child was in a severe car accident? I still had Tori's home number programmed into my phone.

"Hello?" Tori's dad said, in a jovial manner. "Anybody there?"

"Yes, sir. It's Perry Skky."

He said, "Perry! What's up, boy? My daughter's not here right now but I'll tell her you called, okay?"

"Sir." I paused, unable to find the right words.

"Yes? What's going on? Perry?" Tori's father tensed up.

"I'm with your daughter right now, sir."

"All right. What's going on?"

"She and her friends were in a car accident."

"Oh, my gosh."

"She's okay, though. They're taking her to the hospital. I wanted to call so you and your wife can come down there."

"We're on our way. Thanks."

As I watched the ambulance leave, I went over to Damarius and Cole. There were about seven emergency personnel trying to get Ciara out of the car.

"It's going to turn into a ball of fire any minute, man," Damarius said to me.

Finally they pried the door off and grabbed her frail body. "Okay, let's get this young woman out now."

They pulled Ciara out and as hard as Cole and I tried to hold Damarius back, he made his way to her bloody body. The paramedics were saying that she had fatal injuries and she was pronounced dead before Damarius touched her hand. My friend wailed out the loudest, most horrifying cry I had ever heard. All I could do was go over to him and we both fell onto the ground crying.

As I cried with him, Cole came over and wrapped his arms around both of us. I knew none of us would ever be the same, especially Damarius, after seeing someone he loved die.

~ 9 ~

Wishing Life Back

"Come on, Ciara! You gotta come back to me, baby! I'm so sorry I said those things. You know I love you; please forgive me! I wasn't thinking straight," Damarius cried over her lifeless body.

"You guys need to go and get your friend," a paramedic said to Cole and me.

Even though I badly didn't want to, I knew I had to. I wanted him to talk her back to life as the prince did with Sleeping Beauty when he placed a kiss on her cheek. I knew that was a fairy tale and it was wishful thinking but why couldn't it come true? This just didn't seem right. Ciara was just holding on to his leg begging him not to leave her and now she was gone!

Cole said, "Come on, Perry. Let's go and get him. He can't stay over there like that."

Before we could get Damarius, Ciara's mom came running through the crowd, weeping hysterically. "Where's my baby! I gotta see my baby!"

Damarius turned around and ran into her arms. "It's all my fault. This is all my fault!"

"You were driving? I thought they said that she was driving."

"She was driving but I told her I was leaving her right before."

"Boy, you can't blame yourself for this." The two of them held each other.

"I gotta go to the hospital," Cole said. "I need to tell Briana. I don't want her to hear about this from somebody else."

Then I thought about Tori. I knew I had to be there for her too. But it was crazy because I didn't wanna leave my boy in the middle of all his anguish. All of this was too hard. Damarius's dad wasn't too far away. He'd been at the game to witness his son's poor performance. When I got him on the phone and told him what was up, he said he'd turn around and encouraged me and Cole to head to the hospital.

But I stayed with my boy another ten minutes. I just couldn't up and leave. I was there when they covered Ciara with a thin white cloth. I was there when they loaded her body onto the gurney and into the ambulance. I was also there to witness her mother's and Damarius's unbearable sadness. So it was fitting that I was there to witness Damarius's dad do something that he had barely done all of his son's life. And that was hold him in his arms and love him. Seeing them arm in arm made me feel easier about heading to the hospital.

Neither Cole nor I said anything to each other. What do you say at a time like this? "Oh, I'm so glad that our girls are still alive?"

Cole flipped out on me saying, "Man, you need to speed up so we can get to the hospital faster. I don't want Briana to hear about Ciara from somebody else. Hurry up, Perry!"

"And what's that gon' do? Cause another accident with us two? That's real smart."

I could barely see as we got closer to the hospital. Not only was the fog getting heavier as midnight approached, but my eyes were swollen from my waterworks during the last couple of hours.

"I'm sorry, man. I didn't mean to snap at you," I said to Cole, knowing that we both needed to be strong to get through this.

"Yeah, man, me too. Let me hold your cell so I can give my folks a heads-up 'cause I know I'm gon' be late for curfew."

"Your parents still give you a curfew? Man, you 'bout to go off to college."

"I know, right. My dad said until I get there I still gotta live by his rules. And with situations like these, we all need our parents to be strict on us."

After Cole had called his folks I called mine. "Perry?" my mom said when she answered the phone. "I got a call from one of our friends saying that there was an accident at the school. Are you all right?"

"Yeah, mom. I'm all right. But then again I'm not all right."

"They said it was girls in the car and one of them died. Did you know the young ladies?"

"Mom, it was Tori, Ciara, and Briana."

"Oh, my gosh! No!"

"What? What's going on?" I heard my father say in the background.

"Is Tori okay?"

I guess that was the best way you could ask which girl died. My stomach was twisting in all kinds of knots telling her that Tori was fine and explaining about Damarius's girlfriend. I told her I was going to the hospital and then heading home. My mom asked me one final time if I was okay and I knew I wasn't. But to be the man I was trying to be, I didn't wanna spread panic.

"I'm fine, Mom. Cole's with me."

"You all right?" Cole said, as he saw me shaking.

"I don't know what I would've done if something happened to Tori."

"We all knew you still loved her."

"I don't know, man. I just didn't realize what a hard time she had been going through."

"So what you gonna do about it?"

"Right now I just wanna hold her and help her get through the loss of her best friend and assure her that I'll be here. I can't promise her anything, Cole. Who knows what will happen.

By the time I got to the emergency room, Tori had been cleaned up good, but she still had a pretty big gash across her forehead.

"Perry, it's so good to see you."

"No, you're supposed to be resting."

"I can't rest now. What's going on with Ciara?"

I didn't wanna get her upset but when I looked over at her dad, he motioned for me to tell her. I took her hand and told her the terrible news. She leaned into my arms and cried out her heartache. She didn't have to say anything. At that moment, we connected like never before. I knew she was shattered on the inside and she felt that I desperately wanted to hold together whatever I could for her.

"I hate I can't fix it," I said to her.

She just gripped me tighter, letting me know that she appreciated I was there. While her parents gave us privacy, our embrace gave us comfort.

The next day, after my workout I met my mom at the hospital. We both wanted to see Tori. She brought her yellow roses and I was happy to see the smile she brought to Tori's somber face. My mother had always been fond of Tori. I know she was bummed when we broke up but she respected the fact that I was young and that there were going to be many more honeys until I settled down.

That didn't take away the fact that she really liked Tori as a person. But when she saw her lying in a hospital bed recovering from a car accident where she lost one of her friends, it broke her heart. It was a little weird with me being in the corner sorta like a fly on the wall, being apart from the conversation.

"We told your parents that it was okay for them to go home and rest because they've been with you all night and we're here now. They just wanna keep you for observation, I hear."

"Yes ma'am," Tori said, trying to fix herself up and hide her face—as if I hadn't already seen it.

"Honey, that boy is excited that you're fine. Trust me, you look good. You need to concentrate on nothing more but getting well."

"I can't believe we were drinking, Mrs. Skky. I shouldn't have let her get behind the wheel. She had the most to drink out of all of us. She told us to get in the car and I did. I promise I would give anything to reverse it but I can't and she's gone!"

Something inside of me went off. I became so angry, so enraged. I pounded the wall with my fists, scaring my mom a bit, but I didn't care.

"Son, are you okay?"

"No, Mom. I gotta get outta here!"

I got in the car and drove east. I ended up in Myrtle Beach a couple of hours later. I walked on the beach and just fell into the sand.

God, what do you want from us? I don't understand why all of this had to happen. And I thought I was through with Tori. I really don't know what I would do if something happened to her.

Then all of a sudden I thought about Damarius. What was my boy doing? How was he handling today? What's going on inside his head? Did he need me there with him? Yeah, I knew that answer. Of course. Though I hadn't resolved things with God. I had no more understanding of what was going on than before. But since I had to help Damarius, I got back in my car and headed home.

My cell phone rang numerous times. Finally, I looked at it and turned it off. I didn't wanna talk to anybody, just wanted to drive in peace. It was evening when I arrived at Damarius's place. Cars were lined up outside his house.

"Hey, Mom," I said to his mother as I walked in the front door and into the crowded living room.

"Only you can talk to him baby 'cause he ain't speaking to none of us. Cole's been with us most of the day but he just left to check on that Briana girl so your timing is right."

I hadn't been in Damarius's room since the beginning of the year when I had felt sick from the alcohol. As I walked down the corridor, I felt sick again but this time with anxiety.

"Man, I ain't in the mood for no company!" Damarius said, as he heard the door opening.

"It's me," I said, hoping I'd get some kind of pass, knowing deep down he didn't want to be alone.

"I know it's you, boy. I heard your voice in there. I appreciate you coming by, I really do, but what's there to say? I should be sitting in somebody's jail."

"What are you talking about?" I said to him as I sat on the trunk in his room.

"I killed her, Perry."

"D, man, no you didn't."

"Come on, Perry. Let's be real. I knew she was tipsy. Since I was strung out myself, I guess I couldn't take her silly sarcasm and let it go. Instead I let Jaboe egg me on and I can't blame him."

"I don't know why you can't."

"Nobody made me smoke anything. I acted like I did last night 'cause that's what I wanted to do. I wanted to be so over-the-top, the macho man. Ticked off at myself now; taking it out on the wrong people. Didn't I hit you?"

"Oh, I almost forgot. That's why it's been so hard for me to chew lately." We both let out a light laugh.

"Seriously, Perry. I appreciate you, man. I just need time."

"Look here," I said when I went to jab him in the shoulder so he could sit up straight. "This hurts and it ain't supposed to feel good."

"I wish it was a doggoned dream or something. I just wish it wasn't real," Damarius said, trying to fight back the tears. "Why would God do this to her? Why my girl? I really loved her!"

"D, I wouldn't want it to be anybody that I know."

"You the Christian. You mean to tell me *you* ain't got no answers for me?"

"No, I ain't got no answers for you."

"Well, when God clears up all of this, you tell me. 'Cause if this is his way of showing love, then I'm ready for hell. I'm about ready to bust a cap in somebody right now. Maybe somebody should just shoot me. Maybe I should just shoot myself!"

My friend got up searching for something in his room. I didn't even know he had a piece. "Man, you got a gun in here?"

"Yeah, man. When you're out here hustling everyday you gotta have something to protect yourself. Fools is crazy."

"D, promise me you won't do something like that."

"Why shouldn't I? At least me and Ciara will be together again. I don't have a scholarship to college like you. And now my girl's gone. What do I got to look forward to? I can't feel like this every day, Perry. So, you don't want me to shoot my-self? Fine. I'll OD then."

"See now you're just talking psychotic."

"Get out, Perry. Get out!"

I didn't know how to respond to this. He was pounding me on the chest. He was threatening to kill himself.

"Would Ciara want you to do this?" I quickly blurted out.

He instantly composed himself and looked up at me. "I would give anything to have her back. I would apologize over and over again."

"But you can't, man. And we can't understand why every-thing happens when it does. The days might be crazy but you gotta be strong. You're a strong brother and you gotta hold on."

He burst into a shower of tears, grabbed my neck and hugged me real tight. I was salty with Our Father but at the same time I was thankful because he allowed the Holy Spirit to speak through me. I really wasn't clear about what I said. When I felt Damarius hug me tighter, I knew whatever I had said had gotten to him. Keeping my partner sane through all this insanity meant everything to me.

After I left his house I immediately called Tori. Her dad told me she was back home but asleep. I told him to please let her know that I was concerned. He thanked me and told me that would mean a lot to her. When I got home my dad was in the kitchen reading a newspaper story about the hor-rible accident.

He stood to his feet and said, "Son, are you all right?"

"No, dad. I'm not all right."

He clasped his hand around my shoulders and said, "Well, hold on 'cause you will be. We'll get through this."

I could only smile and walk away. Heading to my room I

thought about how in the world I was going to get through these next couple of days and the funeral. This was hard. I didn't want it to be that way.

The next few days were a blur. Everyone kept asking over and over was I okay. Of course I wasn't okay. I wasn't fine. I wasn't good. Honestly, I couldn't sleep at night. Just kept seeing images of the car being demolished by the eighteen-wheeler.

Counselors were at school to talk with anyone who needed help through this crisis. Monday and Tuesday of the next week my parents let me stay home. It wasn't like I could concentrate on anything anyway.

Tuesday afternoon my doorbell kept ringing. My mom had told me earlier that she had a lot of errands to run and that I would be on my own. At first I wasn't going to answer but then I realized it might be important.

Dragging myself to the door wearing only my baggy shorts, I saw that the person at the door was Savoy. I wasn't up for any company. I know she heard the news and probably wanted to make sure I was okay. But since she was standing there I couldn't ignore her like I had been ignoring her phone calls.

It wasn't intentional. She was now on the list of people I didn't want to speak to. I used to be excited to look at her angelic face but today I just needed my space and hoped she could understand. I opened the door and said, "Hey babe."

She stood on her tiptoes and reached to give me a big hug. "Hey dude. I've been worried about you."

"I'm just chilling. You didn't have to come way over here to see me."

"Seriously, Perry. You were on my mind and on my heart and you weren't answering my calls. I needed to do something. Everybody at my school is saying that your ex-girlfriend was the girl who was killed. You don't need to be going through this alone."

I knew she was trying to make me feel better. I saw how she was genuinely concerned so I said, "No. Tori survived the crash. She's banged up pretty bad and devastated because the girl who died was Damarius's girl and her best friend. Well one of them."

"Oh my gosh. And everybody at your school saw it. Were you there?"

"Savoy, I'm sorry but I really don't feel like talking about this now. I'm trying my best to get it out of my system. Is that okay with you?"

"To be honest, I thought we were closer than that. You've been through a real tragedy. Just know that I'm here for you when you're ready."

Now, I don't know if she really meant what she said or if she was caking up to me. And I wasn't trying to be rude or anything but I couldn't be whatever it was she wanted me to be. I reached over to her and kissed her on the cheek.

After pulling back from her quickly, I said, "Thanks for checking on me. I'll call you soon."

The fact that Savoy dropped by made me think of Tori and how she was feeling. I'd been so bummed out the last forty-eight hours. I suddenly felt a deep urge to check on her.

"Hey you," she said after answering the phone.

"I've been thinking about you. Just wanted to call and check in."

It was like Tori was really resting and she wasn't sweating me like I expected. I kinda appreciated that.

"My dad told me that you called. I'm sorry that I didn't call you back."

"No, don't worry about it. You didn't have to. I just wanted you to know that . . ." I was silent for a moment.

"You're glad I'm alive?"

"Yeah, I am."

"I know. I feel so thankful that God gave me more time here on Earth. And as sad as I am about Ciara, I'm equally thrilled to be breathing. Does that make me a bad person?"

"No, but you gotta be wiser. We gotta be smarter. We can't take chances with our lives, Tori."

"I know, I know. I've been thinking about that same thing. Are you coming to the wake?"

"I don't want to."

"But you have to. I need your support."

"No, I'm coming, though. I need to be there for D, too."

"Yeah. How's he doing? I only talked to Briana. Either she's calling me crying or I'm calling her all upset."

"He's hanging in there."

"The six of us used to do everything together. When we broke up, my girls teased me talking 'bout that would never happen again unless I did something to win you back."

"I didn't know that they were saying all kinds of stuff to you and making you feel . . . I don't know."

"Like I'm worthless? 'Cause I didn't have the big jock of the school in my life anymore?"

"Well, yeah. I'm not the one who boosts your self-esteem and makes you you. You were special before me. That's why I wanted to be with you. And somewhere down the line, we lost it."

"Well, seeing my girlfriend's head get smashed through the windshield made me wanna be stronger for you," she said, sobbing. "And I don't know how I'm gonna get through tonight and tomorrow if I'm not as strong as I say I am."

"Don't worry. We'll get through this together," I said to her, meaning it from the bottom of my heart.

As tough as this was for me, I know it had to be tougher

for Damarius and Tori. And dang it, I was certainly not going to let them down. I couldn't bring Ciara back but I could strengthen my friends' spirits and help them through.

During the wake, I successfully did just that. Neither of them wanted to say anything when the reverend asked if any of the friends wanted to speak on Ciara's behalf. So I went and stood behind the podium in the crowded funeral home, looking down at the casket. I so wanted to look over at the crowd and see Ciara's face. But all I saw was a bunch of my peers, devastated. Sad. Sobbing. Down. And I knew just what words of encouragement to say.

So I said nothing more than what I felt in my heart. "Whether you knew Ciara or not, most of us in here are her age. We think that we have so much time to live because we're young, like we're invincible. But when we binge on drugs and alcohol, we are quickly wiped out. She was a girl who loved. She was a girl who spoke her mind. As I look at my closest friends sitting on the front pew, I remember times the six of us shared. Ciara would be the one with the most sense and made decisions that stood for something. She was a leader and I learned something from her. I know if she was here right now she would want us to realize that we're not perfect in this life and we'll make mistakes. But we can learn from those mistakes and improve our lives. If she was standing beside me, I know she would also tell us to be smarter and make wiser decisions, have fun and enjoy yourself, but don't get in over your head."

Now I was getting all emotional thinking about my missed friend. And when I saw Damarius go up to the casket, my heart sank. When Tori wailed out, "Why?" my mind yelled with her. Though I didn't understand what God was doing I know he cared. He cared because I remembered the day she was baptized. Yeah, she may have backslid a little bit, but her salvation was intact.

So I said, "Tori, Damarius. I know it may hurt right now but what would Ciara say? She would want us to not weep, but to live on for her. She's with God in heaven. And from what the Bible said about heaven, she wouldn't return if she could. We gotta be strong and stop wishing life back."

~ 10 ~

Readjusting My Faith

Being at the burial of a dear friend was devastating to me. My heart was beating faster than it ever had, just like at an intense game.

Lord, I thought inwardly as I saw my friends grieving, *I believe you care and I know you love us. I just can't see how or why this is for my good. What did you need that girl up there for? There were so many other angels you could've picked, not that I wanted anyone else to feel what I feel. But dang! It really hurts. Don't you see her mom crying? Can't you understand her pain, knowing that she will never be able to look at or hold her daughter again? Tori and Briana are* devastated *knowing that a piece of their heart is now broken. Damarius is torn and I know that he will never be whole again. This is hard.*

Different people started to place flowers on the casket. When Tori got up there, she just broke down sobbing. Her parents tried to console her but it wasn't working. I moved from behind the crowd to comfort my girl.

"Tori! It's okay, it's okay," I said as I rubbed her back.

"No, it's not Perry," she said as she fell into my arms. "Perry, I gotta get outta here." Tori turned to her father and said, "I can't take this anymore, Dad."

"We're gonna go over to Ciara's house and show our respects to her family."

I said, "Sir, I could stay with her and make sure she's okay. I'll get her to Ciara's house in a bit."

"Thanks. She seems to be responding to you. Take care of my little girl and call me if you need to." I nodded.

Before I could leave with Tori, my dad came through the crowd and asked, "Son, are you okay?"

I just shrugged my shoulders at him. I couldn't explain what I was feeling but I knew that I wasn't feeling too good. How do you say goodbye to someone you love for good?

"Tori is taking it kinda hard and I told her parents that I would give her a ride."

"Are you okay to drive?" my father asked as he placed his hand on my shoulder, squeezing it to show that he cared. I gently touched his fingers, reassuring him that the two of us were cool. "All right, P. Go ahead and do your thing."

"Look out for Damarius, Dad."

"Thanks, Mr. Skky." Tori said, mascara all over her weary face.

After driving around for about twenty minutes in silence I spoke up and said, "Where do you wanna go?"

"It doesn't matter, Perry. Wherever you wanna go is fine. I wish I was dead too so I wouldn't feel this much pain."

We were close by my house so I accelerated the gas a little. I rushed into the driveway so fast that Tori was practically in my lap. I didn't realize that she didn't have her seatbelt on and after the horrific accident that we had just gone through, we both should have been more careful.

But I didn't scold her. I just cupped her pretty face in my hands and said, "Don't say that. What would I do without you?"

Instantly my lips found Tori's and we kissed passionately. I had no thought of anything except that this felt good and suddenly I wasn't feeling so bad anymore. I wanted to sop up every piece of Tori as if she were a biscuit.

She pulled away from me and said, "Perry, what am I gonna do now? My best friend is gone! Briana and I are so broken that we can't talk to each other. I feel so empty and you can't confuse me like this! You can't kiss me; we don't even go out anymore!"

"But I realized after all of this that I love you," I said, drawing her back to me.

We spent the next few minutes fogging up my car windows. Instantly, my manhood started to rise. Tori helped me out of my suit jacket and loosened up my tie. When she unbuttoned my top collar I said, "Let's go inside."

"But your parents—"

"They won't be back for a while."

I led her inside and upstairs to my bedroom. I realized that she had never been there, even though we had been together for the past three years.

"Your room is so high-tech and big! It's wonderful!"

"Who cares about that?" I said as I bent down low and let my hand slide up her left thigh.

I couldn't believe how easily the dress she was wearing came off as she put both her arms in the air and I pulled it off from bottom to top. I was thinking that I had easy access to do whatever I pleased with her but there were plenty more articles of clothing to remove.

"It's just my upper slip, lower slip, stockings, and my underwear," she said, as I looked confused.

She lay down on my bed and began undressing in front of me. When I saw her bare body I was in awe, thinking of what a dummy I'd been to let her go. Putting all that aside, the two of us were here together with only one thing on our minds. I hopped onto the bed so fast that I made her jiggle. And after what we'd both gone through it was nice that we could share some happiness.

I tugged her gently, to my side. Before we went any further, I opened the nightstand and tore open the small square wrapper containing a condom. I had practiced a couple of times so if I was ever in this situation, I wouldn't look too stupid. I slid it on effortlessly and gently slid on top of her. I realized that maybe it wouldn't be so bad to rethink my commitment to wait.

About an hour later after the passion had ended, I held Tori in my arms and just felt sick in my gut. What in the world had I just done? How could I allow my flesh to take control of me? I looked up at my ceiling and thought, *Lord, do you hate me now?*

"Mmm, it felt so good," Tori said to me as she caressed my chest.

I moved her hand away. "I'm tired, girl."

"Tired? That was my first time ever. I got so much energy that I could do this again and again and again."

She reached up and kissed me and I couldn't pull away. I didn't want her to think that it didn't feel good because it felt great, but now my conscience was back.

"Ooh," Tori moaned a little as she slid from under the covers.

"Hey, did I hurt you?" I asked with concern. I felt terrible about what she and I had done. I did care for her and I did love her. But I know God didn't want us to do that. And, I still had feelings for Savoy, which really confused me 'cause I hadn't thought about her at all lately. Now I couldn't take back what I just did.

"Oh, no. You didn't hurt me," Tori explained. "It hurt a little but it felt good after that and I really wanted you. Are you okay, Perry?" she asked. I sat on the edge of the bed, still covered, looking down. "Please don't tell me that you wanna break up again."

How could I respond to that? I never said we were back together. What has this act committed me to? I needed to go to the bathroom and clean up.

"No, it's cool. I'm straight." I leaned back around and kissed her on the cheek. It felt like any gesture or any sort of affection would make her ease up and feel less insecure. Even though she wasn't way off with her accusation, 'cause I was distant. I just couldn't explain it, but all of a sudden I wished I'd never gone there.

Keeping it real while I was in the bathroom, I had to inspect the condom. I felt some kind of confidence when I looked in the mirror. "Go Perry! You made her scream, boy." But were we wrong for allowing our grief to evolve into passion? And now that the moment was over, did our grief count?

It was like some kind of drug. We wanted to get a fix so that we could erase all of our troubles and live our fantasies. Now that reality kicked in, I still felt angry that Ciara is gone. And now Tori was thinking that she and I were now a couple, an item. She also thought this sex thing was the start of something new. To me it was a one time thing, I guess.

Or maybe I would want her again tomorrow. I just knew at that second that I hated myself for what I'd done. I didn't even know if Tori would be able to handle my true feelings. Did I like her better than Savoy? No. Did I want to be Savoy's man, even though I needed space to deal with my loss? Yes. Was there a way that I could fix this? I truly had no idea and that made me really lost. Then there was a knock at the door.

"Perry, let me in! I need to clean up too."

"Are you dressed?" I said before opening the door, not wanting to be turned on again.

"Well, open up and see."

The way she said that let me know that she was nowhere near decent. "Come on, Tori. My parents will be home any second."

"Oh my gosh! I forgot all about that." All of a sudden I heard the pitter-patter of feet run back toward my bedroom.

When I was done I knew I needed to put the same clothes back on before I took her over Ciara's house where her folks were. Where my folks were. Where the whole town was. And if either of us looked any different, who knew what the rumors would be.

On the way back to the repast, I said to Tori, "We really need to talk about what just happened here. You said we were back together and all."

"So is that why you're all uptight?"

"I'm not uptight."

"Yes, you are. Every since, you know, you became weird. Just shut me out. I thought you said you loved me. Did you not mean it?"

"Yeah I meant it."

"So what then?"

"I just don't wanna take things so fast. I told you I was seeing somebody else. I can't just drop all that."

"Wait a minute, Perry. Have you been like *that* with her?"

Whether I did anything with Savoy was none of Tori's business nor did the fact that I let her share a special part of me mean that she was privy to all parts of my life. Again I was so confused.

We pulled up as close as we could to Ciara's house. Cars were lined up everywhere. It was like the whole school, the town came to show love and sympathy. I didn't feel like talk-

ing anymore. Like, what else was there to say? But Tori didn't
let me off that easy.

"No, you can't go anywhere. We got to finish this. Do you
love me, Perry, or is what we just shared not real?"

"I love you. Over everything you should know that."

"Okay, then that settles it. You know what you need to do
with that other chick. We're back together. You can't sleep
with me and just think that it's over. That's outta the question."

I couldn't do anything but stare and scratch my head. I
couldn't believe that she was playing it her way. But she wasn't
backing down and I didn't want to argue with her or have
her break down in more tears right before we walked into
the house.

"I hear you," I told her.

"All right. See I knew I could count on you. I believe that
you love me and I love you. We're gonna be okay."

After all that we'd been through that day, was being okay
even an option?

It was now the end of March and the temperatures were
heating up in Georgia. My dad wanted to take me to the golf
course to have some man time. I wasn't that up for it but I
knew he wasn't taking no for an answer. I felt a little better
when Dakari and his dad tagged along. I was quiet when we
had played the first two holes.

Dakari said, "Why don't Perry ride with me in the cart?
We'll let the real men lead."

"All right now," my dad joked back with him. "Don't kill
my son 'cause you know he gonna be a Yellowjacket. The
Bulldog in you might wanna strike up some competition before he even hit the field."

"No, sir. That's not my job anyway. I'll let the defense handle this good-looking wide receiver. Man! If I had your frame

when I was a freshman, I would've done damage. You look like that and you haven't even started, you gonna get 'em! And you going to Tech, dang we missed out."

"Dakari, you crazy man."

"Don't lose faith, brother. You have to believe in yourself."

"Don't lose faith? Right."

"You tripping a li'l bit 'cause of what happened to your friend?"

"You know about that, huh?"

"Everybody knows about that. You're a strong believer."

"I don't even feel like you do. I mean, I didn't lose a relative, a big brother, or somebody I idolize but this is the first time that I ever lost someone that I was close to. She had so much going for her, you know? And God is up there, how can he allow this to happen?"

"Of course I know. It still hurts sometimes, especially around football season. That was my brother's favorite time of the year. And now I just imagine him playing up in heaven. I was bitter for a long time. I thought I could do a much better job but he broke me. God made me see, and I can't even understand why He does what He does, but only He can ease my pain.

"Some days I'm better than others when I think about heaven being a perfect place. Although I didn't know that my brother gave his life to the Lord, I figured that he did. And I wanna make sure from now on that I don't have to guess about people's salvation and I can know that they heard the gospel because I was the one to share it with them. Never mind."

"No, I hear you. God had to tweak me and maybe he wants to tweak you."

We got out of the cart at the third hole. Our fathers were laughing at something. Dakari really gave me something to think about. As I sat there on the pretty green and looked up at that blue sky, I thought, *Okay, Lord. You wanna fix me, mold me, and make me better? Look in my heart.*

The wind began to blow. It was like an answer from the sky saying, *I heard you, I'm with you and I know what you're going through.*

How can you still love me, Lord, when I slipped up? I did stuff my way. And with Tori, she keeps calling fifty thousand times. I don't even know how to face how I feel. I'm ashamed. What can you do with me? I'm questioning what you allowed to happen. I'm angry.

And in perfect timing, a butterfly landed on my shoulders and flapped its wings. And then flew back up to the sky. And in that moment I felt like the Lord was telling me that angels are watching me all of the time and that He loves me not for who I am but because of who He is.

When I stepped up to the tee, one stroke took me from fourth place to first. My ball got real close to going in. On the second shot, it went in. Everyone had to take five, seven, or nine attempts. I believed that this was God's way of telling me that I could do anything. Even make a hole-in-one. He did make me feel brand-new again after my sexual fall.

When I got back into the cart with Dakari and we rode to hole four, I had a smile on my face. Like God and I were in a conversation that felt so good. I just felt better.

Dakari noticed it and said, "So, what's up? You and God were talking, huh?"

"Dang, how you know?" I had to laugh when I looked over and saw him put his visor on backwards and lean out the cart like he was profiling.

"Don't be hating, for real. You know you like my driving. I better sit up straight and act like I got some sense before my dad start acting crazy."

"I know, right," I agreed. "Plus, you black and you out here. You can't be acting silly out here."

"They know who we are. I play ball on a college level. The best players they had were coming out of our school. And my dad got bank. Oh, we different kinda Negroes."

"And Lucy Laney didn't teach me that lesson."

"Wait until next year, you'll see what I mean."

I looked back up at the sky and thought, *Lord, you know what, hurdles and obstacles don't matter, bring it on. By now I know You love me and I feel Your presence. I believe Your word when You said goodness and mercy would follow me, support me, guide me, challenge me, and encourage me.*

"Yeah, Perry life is tough. But I learned that when you let God be a part of it all then it's like a big defensive lineman, it's all talk and no action. Any more problems you needed me to solve?" Dakari punched me in the arm and we both started laughing.

"Ow, man! You are trying to hurt me. That's my catching arm. I take the ball with this one."

"Yeah, I know. I was trying to mess Tech up but you caught me. Dang!"

"Do you ever get nervous out there on the field?"

"Yeah. But like I just said, pray about it. Let God worry about the stuff inside that just rattles you."

"So what about sex and stuff like that?"

"What about it? You finally slipped, didn't you?"

What was it? Did I have a sign on my forehead that said, "Virgin no more?"

"You're wondering how I know, huh? Let it ride, man. There's going to be plenty of girls that throw themselves at you when you play ball. I remember when we were in school, you know, my senior year."

"You mean that fight we almost had in the middle of the hallway when you embarrassed my sister?"

"You understand now, huh? When somebody's ready to give it up and your sister was keeping her legs closed?"

"Yeah, all right, man."

"So, what, you're struggling with dealing with the flesh?" I just sat there. "Okay, I'll take your non-answer as a yeah."

"Well, yeah."

"I want you to know that it's a daily struggle for me, being that it's my sophomore year in college. I'm unattached so I don't have to worry about breaking some girl's heart."

"I guess that's my dilemma."

"You didn't cheat on your girl did you? Just like me back in the day and you got all up in my face."

"I know right. And it's weird because I was with my ex. You didn't even know the girl you did my sister wrong for."

"Oh, I knew her all right."

"See, you crazy." Then I punched him in the arm.

I liked talking to him. Having somebody I could talk to and be honest with. And then I liked that my sister was with Tad 'cause I didn't have to worry about him dogging her. Dakari was a little more my speed and he could help me break through the challenges that I faced.

"The only thing I can tell you is pray, man," he said before we stepped out of the cart again. "Ask God what does he want from you. Is it the ex-girlfriend, new girlfriend, no girlfriend? Don't lay all of that drama on yourself. You gotta Heavenly Father there to guide your steps. I love listening to gospel music when I'm at a crossroad. Like Donnie McClurkin says, 'We fall down but we get up.'"

"I believe it. When your faith get so strong, you begin to stumble. Just get back up again. Make love to God, you know? It may sound crazy but when you stray from Him, you act a fool. There are plenty of times that I come out here to the course and let nature talk to me. And I look at that as getting back on track to do the best that I can. Gotta keep readjusting my faith."

~ 11 ~

Losing Builds Character

It's one thing to shut the world out. But it's a completely different thing when someone shuts you out. You feel on edge. You wonder what's going on. You wanna reconnect.

A week had gone by since my intimate experience with Tori. Now I was really missing Savoy. I called her a few times but she never picked up. I left messages and she never returned them. It didn't take me long to understand that she would put me down just as I had previously shut her out.

I guess I just had to chalk up my inconsistency to being an eighteen-year-old teen. I was at my prime. A few more months and I would be off to college, into the real world. Decisions were going to be tough everywhere I looked. No wonder it was hard to choose which girl I wanted to be with.

I've never wanted to play either of them. I finally understood what Cole and Damarius raved about for so long. Sometimes one woman just won't do it. And since Savoy had shut me out, honestly, she was more desirable than ever.

Things at my school had gotten back to normal. Maybe normal wasn't the right word. People just didn't seem so sad all the time anymore, except for Damarius. He hadn't even come back to school yet. Talk about cutting a brother out of your life. He wasn't even staying at home. He had gotten tired of people calling asking about Ciara. I guess it was too hard on him. He went to stay with his grandmother in D.C.

Cole and I never were too hype about three-way. But we decided to call Damarius up and see when he was going to return. But he wouldn't answer us. I knew I needed to think of something to get him out of this rut, but what? How? Where could I take him to make him forget his pain? I just wanted to hear his voice because whenever he needed me, I'd be there.

At the lunch table, everybody was making plans for the prom. I was glad that Tori and I didn't have the same schedule. I wasn't ignoring her. I just needed to put some distance between us. However, I looked up and saw that she was heading my way. What was she doing in the cafeteria at this hour?

She came over and nudged my arm. "I got out of class to come to your lunch. Do you see everybody planning for the prom?"

"Yeah. So?"

"Well you haven't asked me yet."

I already knew what that was about and I set myself up for it. But she wasn't going to get me twice. I wasn't going to just give in and say we were going together. I still had a girlfriend. At least I thought I did. I mean, I know Savoy and I haven't talked but she couldn't be through with me, could she? Wasn't I supposed to escort her to her prom and vice versa? I was nowhere near trying to take Tori.

"Can we talk about this later? I'm hungry and I gotta head to class in a minute," I said, trying desperately to change the subject.

"I just wanted to make sure we were going together. You haven't mentioned it and I still have to get a gown. My mom has been asking me about it and so has my dad. I mean, are you taking me or what?"

"Oh, here we go. The pressure again."

"Why everytime I say something you don't like, Perry, I gotta be pressuring you?"

"Why you gotta get all loud?" I said to her as I realized how much her voice escalated when people began staring at us. "Forget it. If you gon' be all crazy, I'll just talk to you later."

"No, wait," she said.

And I hated playing that card with her. But I hated looking like some weak punk even more.

"I'll call you tonight so we can talk about it," I said to her before heading to class.

After school, I was hanging out with Cole in the gym and my cell phone rang. I don't know why but I just knew it was Tori. Didn't I tell her I'd call her tonight?

I looked at Cole and said, "I just want a little break."

"Well, from what Briana told me about you two, you won't be getting a break soon. Why you ain't tell me man?"

Now this wasn't cool. Cole was one of my best friends but I still didn't want my business to be all out.

"I thought good girls don't kiss and tell," I said to my friend. "You can't believe everything you hear."

"Perry, please. You can look at that girl and see how sprung she is over you. You had to hit her with something and I know it wasn't your fist. She gon' keep calling."

I was actually surprised when I saw Savoy's name pop up. "Hey you," I said.

"Oh. So that's how you play someone you don't wanna talk to," Cole said in the background. I swatted my hand at him to make him shut up.

"Savoy, hey." I responded into the receiver, so Cole would stop messing up my game.

"Dang, my bad! I thought it was Tori. Let me call Damarius 'cause I know he'll answer now. I didn't know you was swinging it like that, P. Play on player."

"Who is that in the background?"

"Just a bunch of boys in the locker room. They ain't talking 'bout nothing," I said, trying to play it off, wishing I could tell my boy that I didn't roll like that. But instead I walked over to a corner for some privacy. "So you finally getting back to me, huh?"

"No, I was trying to give you some time, like you said. I got all your messages. You must have missed me or something?"

"Well, what do you think? You wasn't calling me so I had to call you."

"I think I remember differently. I remember coming over to your house to check up on you and you brushed me off. Yet you miss me? Please. I don't believe that. I decided not to call you ever—until now."

"Oh, come on babe. It was hard and I was frustrated. But when I did wanna talk to you and you didn't call me back it made me long to hear your voice. You still care about me, right?"

"Should I? I've had so much stress lately. You wouldn't even understand it all."

"Try me."

"I've been getting ready for track."

"Oh, that's right. I can't wait to come to a meet."

"You're really gonna come?"

"Well, yeah. You know I can't wait to see my girl do her thing."

"Perry, you know you can talk to me. You've been through too much to try and shut me out. Always know I'm here for you."

"I know. I mean, I didn't know how to deal with comforting my best friend, comforting Tori, and making sure I was okay."

"Wait. Why would you have to comfort your ex?"

"Well, the girl who died was her best friend."

"Oh. Well I hate that had to happen. And I know she needs you now. It's prom time and all that. Go with her and make sure she has fun. You gon' take me to mine, right? You're not the only one who missed the other here. I wanna make it better. This is your senior prom and I would love to be on your arm for you to show me off, but there will be other events."

"You mean the debutante ball?"

"Yeah, and two others. My prom and your Beautillion. So that'll make three big events."

"Well, I'll take her and be thinking of no one else but you."

"I know."

Wow. I was amazed. Savoy had helped me solve my own problem. But had I dug a deeper hole for me to get out of? I never knew that absence really does make the heart grow fonder. She was special and I recognized that.

It certainly wasn't hard for me to tell that it was April, with all the rain that was coming down. I didn't have a problem with the rain or the cold—I liked all weather that God created. But sometimes I wanted a break.

I sloshed through the rain from my car to the house. When I walked in, my mom had a list of things for me to do so I put off calling Tori.

"Boy, you're almost off to college next year. And it's just a hot mess that you can't keep your room clean. You have to straighten up the garage. And the basement could use a touch-up as well. Quit moping and take care of things."

"I'm all right, Mom. I hate that I lost a friend, but it made me stronger."

"That's good, sweetie." She came over and gave me a big hug.

I'm not a little boy anymore, but I realized in her embrace

how much she cared about me and how much I'll miss her next year. Every time I thought about how short Ciara's life was I realized I had no clue when mine would end—or anyone's that I cared about. So I didn't wanna take stuff for granted anymore. I hugged her back.

"My baby's a grown man."

When the day finally settled down but before it got too late, I dialed Tori up. She answered in a not-so-nice tone.

"Oh, come on now. I know you're not mad at me," I reasoned, feeling like I'd gone above and beyond by telling her what she wanted to hear even though that wasn't how I felt.

"How do you expect me to feel Perry? You say we're back together but yet you treat me like I'm a pest sometimes. I always have to do what I say or feel on your time. That's just not fair."

"Do you wanna go to the prom with me or not?" I said, not wanting to deal with all of the whining.

"You know I wanna go with you. What kind of question is that?"

"Well let's do it then," I replied with a little hostility.

"Don't get mad at me!"

"I'm not mad at you. I'm just still worried about Damarius."

"How's he doing?"

"I don't know. I talked to his mom and she said she didn't know when he was coming back."

"Losing Ciara is tearing him apart, huh?"

I relaxed back in my bed. "Looks that way. And I don't know what else to do besides be there for him."

"Spring break's coming up. Maybe y'all could take a trip somewhere."

"He wouldn't wanna go anywhere with me. And Cole would probably wanna bring his girl."

"Briana wouldn't wanna go with y'all. It would be a boys' thing. Have you broken up with that girl from Aiken yet?" Tori questioned.

I suddenly became quiet. There was no way I could answer that question truthfully. I didn't wanna be caught in a lie but saying nothing was just as bad. I didn't wanna go a step further than that. Something implied is one thing, but something said is something else. I couldn't break her heart again. Until I figured out how I was gonna deal with this situation myself, I was gonna play it cool.

"Perry, I was just saying. I didn't mean to get you uptight."

"I know. I wish you would just back off of that stuff. We're together. We're going to the prom aren't we? Why can't you be happy with that?"

"I am. I'm so excited. All I've been thinking about was being in your bed. Me rolling my hips for you."

"Don't talk like that, girl."

"What! Don't you think about it too?"

"I just don't know if that was right."

"What do you mean? It felt great. I love you, and it just didn't feel wrong."

"It felt wrong to me. We have to keep praying about it and allow God to lead us to what's next for us in that area."

"Well, I already spotted four dresses that I absolutely loved. But my mom didn't buy any until she was sure that I had a date. I'll let you know what color I get so you can order your tux to match."

I didn't care about all that. Whatever color she picked was fine with me. As soon as we hung up I dialed Cole. Sometimes Tori made a lot of sense. The spring break trip was an excellent idea.

After I pitched it to Cole I said, "What you think?"

"Man, that's hot. We need to go to the beach."

"What, Myrtle Beach? Hilton Head?"

"No. We need to get away somewhere other than a neighboring state. Maybe Florida."

"Boy, Florida borders Georgia too."

"If we're far down there, it won't count."

"How long do you think it'll take D to come back?"

"Man, we'll call up there and tell him we're taking a trip and he'll roll back this way."

"I think he thinks we've been busy with other stuff and he didn't wanna burden us. When he sees we wanna spend time with him, he'll come around. How you and Briana been feeling lately?"

"I guess losing Ciara has pulled us closer. She doesn't have her girl and in a way Damarius is gone from my life. Man, I wanna change that so I'm down for what you're talking 'bout. How much is it gonna cost though? You know a brother is broke these days."

"I'll talk to my dad and see what he come up with."

"You better talk to your rich friend Jordan."

"Yeah. We haven't had classes together this year."

"So call him up. We can spend some of his money. You don't need to put most of this off on your pops. Jordan's cool, right?"

"All right. You work on trying to get Damarius and I'll work on the plans."

"Florida here we come!" Cole said.

"Maybe something good can come out of this trip with what we've been through."

"Partying on the beach with a bunch of pretty girls in bikinis. Oh, yeah. I'm in!"

"You stupid!"

"I'm just playing. We're doing this to bond with our boy."

"We need to build up his spirit. That's why we're going," I said.

* * *

Prom night at Lucy Laney High School was here. At first I hadn't been all excited, but I had to admit once I put on this sweet tailored tux and silver cummerbund, I was hot. I was actually really looking forward to the evening.

Damarius was back. Cole had talked him into making an appearance at the prom. He was going to go with Briana, Cole, Tori, and me. I was more excited when he mentioned that Ciara wouldn't have wanted it any other way. He arrived at my house first. My dad had rented a big limo for us to cruise around in. It was big enough to fit twelve. So we knew we'd hit up the place in style.

"I'm glad to see you, man," I told my boy.

"You know where I was, right?"

"In D.C. at your grandma's."

"No. I was in rehab."

"What?"

"It just been so hard. I was drinking more and smoking a lot. Staying high so I would feel no pain. My grandma pulled me by the ear down to some place. And for ten days it was just me and the walls."

I extended my hand to give him his props. We slapped and then embraced. He had been through more than I could even imagine. It was great to see my friend looking good on the outside in his Armani suit with black accessories.

But now he was also strong on the inside. And that confidence made me glad to know him. It was like God had heard my prayers for my friend. And at his saddest hour, God brought my boy back to me stronger than ever.

"I'm glad you and Cole wanted me to go to be y'all's chaperone at this prom and all."

"Oh yeah. You know we couldn't step into the place without you." I placed a hand on his shoulder. "Are you gonna be all right? I know people are gonna be asking you about Ciara. Are you able to talk about her?"

"Yeah, I'm able to talk about her. I know she's with me and God. That's the only way that could explain all this. He needed another angel with him. She's an angel watching over me. Whether or not she can hear me is beside the point. Maybe I'm just talking to myself. But sometimes I think about her and talk to her and she helps me get a better perspective."

Truly it sounded like that was the Holy Spirit working in his heart. But I didn't wanna bust his bubble. Whatever he needed to help him through this I was all for it. Particularly since there were no drugs involved.

After Cole arrived at our house in his tails, gold cummerbund and tie, my mom had to get several pictures. My dad gave us a big speech about being careful, and in no time we were on our way to get the girls from Tori's place.

Briana's mom was there and we had more photos to take. It actually worked out pretty well. I took pictures with Tori. She looked so beautiful in her tight, silver gown—she made sure my focus would be her. Briana and Cole took a few snapshots. And when Damarius got in between the two ladies, he felt like the man.

Our prom was at the Augusta Civic Center. Driving there, we were quiet. But I knew what everyone was thinking. We all wished that Ciara was with us, like old times. But she wasn't and she wouldn't want us to be sad or bummed out tonight. I knew she was happier with God. For us guys this was our senior prom. We needed to make it special. My dad had stocked the bar with Coke, Sprite, and water. I asked everyone what they wanted.

Damarius said, "I wanna make a toast to you. I know you guys been worried about me. I know you two, Briana and Tori, really miss your friend. Even though y'all ain't saying nothing we all wish she was here with us. So here's to Ciara. A girl who is forever loved."

Tori hugged me and naturally I kissed her.

"Uh, yeah. I'm the chaperone so I'll be needing to sit in between y'all," Damarius said, as he scooted in between us two. We laughed then.

All five of us strolled into the prom together. Different girls came up to Damarius—and there were a lot of girls that had come without a date. Every time I looked over at the boy he was on the dance floor with another female, having a good time being himself.

It was a good thing to know that God could take us through tough circumstances and mold us into better people.

Tori came to me and said, "Your boy sure looks happy. Can we join him on the dance floor?"

We hadn't danced that much. She was mingling with girls here and there. Though in my heart we weren't an item, I enjoyed her seeing her happy. And for real, out of all the chicks in the school, she was my favorite.

As we slow danced I couldn't help thinking about Savoy at home, wondering how my night was going. As I knew my buddy Damarius was maturing and taking responsibility, what could I say about me? When it came to me I couldn't say anything good.

At that point people had been voting for king and queen all night. People had told me all week to get ready for another crown. I had won something for homecoming. I'm not saying it to be mean or anything but I was ready to get it over with. I was actually ready to jet outta the place to go get my grub on. Damarius was with us as a chaperone because Tori and me all alone was not going to happen this night. And not that she wasn't fine and all, but she really deserved a guy to respect her and not to take advantage.

"And our queen for the evening is . . . Amandi Roberts."

That really killed me. I didn't wanna stand on the stage with the girl that ruined me last semester by spreading rumors that I was scared to touch her. She made me out to be a punk. It took a minute, but I got that crap straight. Amandi's outfit was too revealing with the thigh-high split and backless gold gown. She looked like a tramp in my eyes.

"And our king is Damarius Jones."

I was heading to the stage but was glad I stopped in my tracks because they didn't call my name. I saw my friend fly from the back of the crowd to the front. He put on his crown and the whole room cheered. It was like he was a star. And for a split second I didn't believe it, but I found myself cheering too.

What a great way for my friend to know that we were all behind him! That we all felt his pain and that he was a king in our books. And for him to win the crown at our prom—he actually saw the support he had. The king and queen went to the middle of the floor and danced. And as I watched Damarius feel good about himself, I realized that I wouldn't have had this turn out any other way.

This whole thing taught me so much. Like the Word says, "What the Lord giveth, the Lord may taketh away." And in Job, "But in both situations, blessed be the name of the Lord." And I was thankful that God was blessing my friend.

Yeah, I didn't win the crown, but I got something even better. And even Damarius got something more valuable from this. I think we found out that when something you want is gone, you look real hard at the depth of your circumstance. And you can find out that losing builds character.

~ 12 ~

Breaking Down Totally

Spring break was finally here. And to start it off was Easter weekend. Tori and I went out Friday night, and I took Savoy out on Saturday. I felt so guilty with both of them. However, I didn't lose my composure outwardly. I was the first one in church on Easter Sunday ready to repent.

I was also really excited because my boys Cole, Damarius, and Jordan were with me. After service we were set to eat dinner at my place, then head on out for our week's vacation. My mom was not feeling the trip at all. Actually all our mothers were worried about four guys setting out to the coast. The car accident was still fresh in their minds.

So I was thankful when my dad stepped in and defended our need to have an adventure. Plus if they would've tripped, I would've had to pull the "you did it for Payton" card. I remembered they let my sister go on a trip to Myrtle Beach with her friends last spring break. Thankfully, I didn't have to go there.

On Sunday morning, the pastor said, "Y'all look lovely today. I know Easter Sunday is the best-dressed day in every church across America. Amen."

"Amen," the crowd replied collectively.

"If you would, turn to Luke 8:22-25. I don't just want you

to come to church Easter Sunday and look good. I want you to feel good too. And sometimes to be empowered you have to understand what it feels like to be down. Confused. Upset. Shaken. Has anybody out there ever felt like that?"

He got a few more *amens*. I wanted to say it too, but with my boys there I played it cool.

"Has anybody ever felt like God wasn't there? The Lord knows so there's no need to be shy."

So I said, "Amen." Others around me shouted out the same.

"That's what I'm talking 'bout in here. Let's be real in here today."

I didn't even have to look to my left to see what my boys thought. I was here to feel the Word. If I was worried about what any of them thought, I wouldn't be ready to absorb God's word into my life. And I was the first to admit that I had many issues that I needed God to solve.

As we stood and read the scripture together, I remembered the story where Jesus asked his disciples out on a boat to fish with him. But somewhere during the night Jesus fell asleep and the strong winds and storms came. They had to go wake Jesus up and ask him what He was doing. They felt like they were going to die. And Jesus did his thing and there was peace upon the sea.

But I wasn't familiar with the verses the preacher was talking 'bout today. All of that was in verse twenty-five. That verse twenty-five was awesome! I had to reread it myself.

"The Lord said, 'O ye of little faith,'" my pastor quoted. "Today I'm gonna preach on how not to have a breakdown. The first point I wanna say to you all is that when God leads your steps as he did with the disciples, asking them to come with Him, He surely guides you."

Cole elbowed me in the arm. "That's what I'm talking 'bout," my friend leaned over and whispered to me.

It was a shame how much I cared for those jokers, but the last time I had been at a church was at Ciara's funeral. I was glad to know he was listening. A little later on in the message, I took a pen outta my suit jacket and started taking notes. I'd had a lot of breakdowns the last couple of months.

The pastor grabbed the mike from the holder, looked out at the crowd and sternly said, "Every now and then we might struggle with the Holy Spirit. We might begin to question all we know. When a storm comes into your life I just want you to take God your troubles. When you first get to a point where you get scared and get tired of calling on Him, don't worry. He'll never get tired of listening. He listens to us all. Not like some of us who look at the caller ID and if we don't know who it is, we won't answer." The majority of the crowd agreed. I really liked this guy.

"Well I'm not gonna hold us long. I know the kids wanna go and get their eggs. And some of y'all wanna go eat the hog. But with whatever you're about to do, I want you to remember that when God brings you out of the storm, learn something. Church, with this being Easter Sunday, we celebrate the Lord's resurrection."

Damarius stood up and shouted, "Wow! What a message for the four of us."

At three o'clock we were on the road heading to Destin, Florida. We had a long seven-hour drive. Though my parents had told me it was really nice, I wished Damarius would've chosen something a little closer. However we were still excited to take the trip, and he was set on this place.

My dad knew it wasn't realistic for me to drive the whole time. So he was very adamant about getting driver's license copies and insurance information from Cole and Jordan. He approved them to be driving assistants. Damarius didn't have a car of his own and though he could drive, he didn't ask any questions.

The first hour was quite fun. My dad told us how to get there going through South Carolina. He mapped out the hot spots for food, gas, everything. As long as we followed what he told us, we would be straight. Dad was being so precise with his directions, it cracked us up. He even knew our first stop for gas needed to be in Atlanta.

"I'm gonna pay some of this with my card," Jordan said. "We need to look for a BP around here."

"No. Chevron is where we need to go," Damarius said.

"Man, please. If he's paying for the gas then we need to go wherever his credit card is going."

"Well I'm just going to meet my cousin at a Chevron and get some uh, some stuff from him."

The way Damarius was talking was really weird. He was real persistent about going to Chevron. So to keep the peace I said, "Man, I got cash. Let's just go to Chevron. Jordan, you can get it next time."

Damarius said, "Yeah. That's a good idea. Let's go to the Chevron since it's right over there."

Sure enough as I got out to pump gas Damarius dashed outta the car and headed over to a black 1967 Ford. I looked over at the guys with squinted eyes. What the heck was Damarius doing? I saw them shake hands, Damarius came running back with a new cell phone, and the guys drove off. I just had to assume that it was what my friend said it was.

"I didn't know you had any relatives in Atlanta," I told him.

"Man. My dad got people out the woodwork. You know he a rolling stone. My cousin might be my brother."

We both laughed when he got back in the car and continued our trip. We went down I-85 and got to Alabama in no time. When we arrived in Montgomery, Damarius was bugging us again to stop at another specific location. They'd planned to go to QuikTrip but there was a BP close by.

So we stopped at the BP, but Damarius went across the street to the QuikTrip anyway. When he came back with a tasty slushy, what could I say?

"Dang, y'all wanted one? I'm sorry."

We were eating fast food cause we didn't want any more long stops. We were all hyped to get to our hotel room, ready to crash. Again Damarius had the hookup down there and my dad was tied in too. We would end up paying only forty dollars a night.

Cole was driving when Damarius and I got in the back. We must have fallen asleep 'cause I woke up to Jordan saying, "See. I told your tail we should've stopped. Now we're out of gas!"

"Well if you would've woke Damarius up I would've known where to stop."

"Perry said he had cash. I know you ain't come down here with no money. Now we in the backwoods stuck, on the side of the road. You act just like a dumb jock."

Cole quickly unbuckled his seatbelt, threw it across his arms, and was about to punch Jordan in the face.

"Wait a minute. Hold up," I said from the backseat, trying to come between the two of them. But Cole was a large brother. He was the best defensive lineman from our state for a reason. He had skills and size.

Jordan could talk all that junk if he wanted to. But he just didn't know what his mouth was doing. "Like I'm scared of you."

"You need to be scared of me. I'll crush your li'l tail."

Damarius got out of the back and opened the passenger side, pulling Jordan outta the car. He was trying to calm him down. I tried to do the same thing with Cole but it wasn't working.

Cole said, "He calling me dumb. Just 'cause I ain't in them smart classes like y'all don't make me dumb. Shoot. I got a scholarship to college. Does his tail know where he going?"

"Man, he didn't mean that, I said, trying to defuse the tension. "We need to put all of this bull aside and think how we gonna get out of this mess."

"If he just stopped when I told him to stop about ten miles back, we wouldn't be in this situation," Jordan blabbed, not knowing when to shut up.

"You better shut up before I—" Cole said before being cut off.

Jordain said, "I ain't scared, man."

I pointed to Damarius and Jordan and said, "Y'all two need to walk to the gas station. We'll wait here, till y'all get back."

"Oh, no," Jordan said. "I ain't walking nowhere 'cause I told him he needed to stop. Cole need to get to walking. Maybe walking a bit will get his big butt in shape."

"Oh heck naw," Cole said as he pulled his arms away from me. He pushed through the car to the passenger side, knocking Damarius into Jordan's gut.

Jordan grabbed his stomach and fell to the ground. Cole wanted to hit him again. It took both Damarius and me to get him to stay back.

I asked, "Dang, D. Can't y'all go get the gas?"

"Uh-uh. I need to stay here with my, uh, stuff," Damarius replied nervously.

"What you mean?" I asked. "Me and Cole got it. And they need some time apart to cool down."

Damarius said, "All right. Well, I'll stay here with Cole and you go with your buddy. We don't even know that dude."

"Oh, it's like that?" Jordan said from the ground. "Y'all athletes sticking together now? I knew I shouldn't have come.

We ain't even been hanging all semester but he invites me on the trip to help pay 'cause y'all broke, right?"

"Okay, okay. Let's all just calm down," I said. "Come on, Jordan."

I was mad at all of them, but we were all stuck with each other for the next four or five days. Thankfully, two miles down the road we found a gas station. The country owner was kind enough to give us a ride back to our car.

Once we put a little something in the tank, we turned around and headed back to the station to fill up. We still had a little ways to go to get to our destination. By the time we got back on the road we all were mentally beat down. Nobody said a word.

When we arrived in Destin, all four of us perked up. There were kids everywhere—hanging out in cars, walking the beach. It was just light enough to see the white sandy beaches that my parents told me were so beautiful.

"So what we gon' do first y'all?" I said after checking into our place.

I couldn't believe the two-bedroom suite. I was ready to get my grub on. Cole and Jordan wanted to go get their groove on at the beach. Damarius kept making excuses about just chilling. He's been so weird that I finally had a strong gut feeling that he was up to something.

Cole and Jordan kept mugging at each other. I thought it was so juvenile of them. The two of them needed to quit tripping, so I said, "House meeting."

"House meeting? What the heck is that?" Damarius asked. "I just wanna chill and make a couple of phone calls. Dang, Perry. We don't have to do everything on your schedule."

"We came down here following yours. What's up, partner, we can't talk?"

"All right. Go ahead. What you wanna say? We only came down here to have a good time. We don't need to do everything together," Damarius said.

"I just wanna pray. That's all. We need to put God back on our itinerary 'cause we have a lot of tension on our hands. And I don't know how we're going to be able to live under the same roof with all this foolishness."

The three of them finally looked at me with respect. If I knew that all I needed to say was "God" then I would've brought Him into it a long time ago. Now they acted like they had some sense. So, asking them to bow their heads, I spoke the truth.

"Lord. We just need a little help right now. Help getting along, help for this week, and help living our lives the way You want us to. Before we have a breakdown, I'm just asking for some help. Amen."

All three of them chimed in and responded, "Amen."

Then Jordan said, "Cole, I owe you an apology for saying what I said about you."

"No, man. I shouldn't have hit you. You wouldn't wanna fight somebody twice your size. You all right?"

"Yeah, I'm straight. Let's go hit the beach and get with some of these girls up here."

"You right. Let's go get some honeys!"

"Say, man. You gonna go with me to get something to eat?" I asked Damarius.

"If you wanna bring me something back, that's cool. But I just want some me time for a few. We were all bunched up in a car together. I wanna chill alone. I don't wanna be in a car no more."

"They got all kinds of restaurants within walking distance."

"All right. Well let me take a shower and I'll think on it."

"I need to take a shower too."

When I got out the shower I decided to ask Damarius one

final time to get some food with me. It had been thirty minutes and I knew that was enough time for him to decide. I was surprised to find my buddy counting little packets of white powder. His back was to the door but I heard him speaking.

"Yeah, I made the other drops. I just got to deliver this down here. My partners don't know nothing so you ain't gonna have to hurt nobody. I'll get it done. I'll hit you later, Jaboe. I gotta go."

When he hung up the phone and threw it on the bed, I pushed the door back and it hit the wall with a clang. I startled Damarius when he turned around. He started gathering his stuff on the bed.

I rushed over to the bed and grabbed a few packets, then ran straight back into the bathroom. I went to the sink and opened one packet, attempting to empty it.

"No, man. You can't pour that out. I'm not taking none of that stuff."

"You said you went to rehab," I said.

"I'm not taking it. It's not mine."

"I heard you on the phone. No wonder you took us the long way. No wonder we had to stop in specific places. Talking 'bout you had relatives and stuff. You took us for fools. You didn't wanna go and get some gas cause you had your drugs in the car."

"That's right. 'Cause if the po-po came I would've made sure they didn't find it. You guys would have been in ice creek by now."

I turned over the pouch and emptied out the first bag of white powder. I turned on the water and let it wash down the drain. I pushed him hard and went back into the room and got more. When I went back the next time, we scuffled.

"You just don't understand, Perry. Things are so perfect for you. You don't know."

"I know it's hard for you. But selling drugs for that punk

makes it better? Remember you were high that night Ciara died."

"Oh, so you just gonna throw that in my face? That's foul, P."

"I need to 'cause it don't seem like you learned nothing."

"Do you know I don't have anything else? I only had a few dollars to get by and the only way I could pay Jaboe back was by selling."

My friend was in tears and let go of my hand holding the five remaining packets. The heck with Jaboe. I didn't care what he had done to me anymore. I cared about Damarius. He was in real trouble and I hadn't done anything besides telling to him to quit his association with that punk. But dang it, I wasn't going to be held hostage anymore. I was going to have to stand up and intervene. I couldn't let my friend continue to live his life this way.

"We gonna find a way," I said to him.

"How we gonna find a way, Perry? I owe him five Gs. You got that?"

"No, I don't have all the answers either. I ain't that completely through with Jaboe either. He got something over my head."

"I know."

"You know?"

"Yeah. He showed me the stupid tape. That ain't right, man. I'm trying to do what I gotta do for myself now, Perry. You gotta understand that. Just 'cause I did wrong doesn't mean you gotta do wrong too. You were right. What I said that night sent Ciara over the edge 'cause I was high."

"I shouldn't have said that."

"Just remember what your pastor said when you feel you're losing self-control. Go to the Lord for help. I need the Lord today, Perry, 'cause I'm breaking down totally."

~ 13 ~

Enjoying Life's Moments

Sitting there on the floor, sobbing with Damarius, meant something to me. He was letting his emotions show 'cause he was tired of holding in the pain. And I was letting the tears loose 'cause I cared about someone else more than I cared about me. It was about time that I let myself feel something deep.

I had been so selfishly worried that Jaboe was going to mess up my reputation that I was willing to let my friend's life spiral out of control. I knew what he had been doing and going through but I hadn't looked after my boy. I had to think of a plan to get Damarius from under Jaboe's reign of terror for good.

I didn't hear Jordan and Cole come in but I was startled by Jordan's joke.

"Group hug."

Cole stepped in and said, "All right man. We're cool now. Don't make me hit you again."

Damarius, Cole, and I had a serious bond. We'd been through a lot over the last four years of high school. Nothing was as traumatic as enduring the last six weeks together. Cole knew Damarius was slipping away from us, and I guess witnessing the solidarity of a hug meant something to him too.

The four of us spent the next hour discussing why Damarius was really down here. We all agreed that we couldn't afford for Damarius to get caught being Jaboe's drop-off man. We vowed that when morning hit, we'd head up to Panama City and enjoy the rest of our spring break.

It was midnight when Damarius's cell phone went off. I looked at my friend staring at it like it was a live grenade or something. But if he didn't pick it up he knew he'd be in even more trouble. I'm sure it wasn't a smart move to make but I picked up the cell phone, and before Damarius could stop me I said, "Hello?"

"Who is this?"

I knew who I was and I knew who he was. So I played it back and said, "Who is this?"

"Oh. You that Perry boy trying to be all big and bad. You know who I am, punk. Now put Damarius on the phone."

"He ain't here."

"Well don't you think you need to go find him and tell him to call me back in a minute? Not five minutes. But sixty seconds. Got that, jack?"

"No, man. We ain't gon' be able to do it. I really can't even hear you; we got a little bit of a bad reception."

"Go get Damarius. Now!" he yelled.

This was my time now to not be a punk. To really dig down deep and be a man. Yeah, Jaboe was a gangster. Yeah, he killed folks with no remorse. Yeah, he had something over me. But it was time for all the running and intimidation to stop.

I said, "Look."

"No, you look. I give the orders. You listen and follow. Got it?"

"No."

"Where are y'all? I need to show you that I run the show and you're not as tough as you think you are. How 'bout if I shove my fist down your throat, pretty boy?"

"Call me whatever you want. Threaten me however you want. I'm gon' tell you how it is now. We got your merchandise."

"He showed you that? Damarius getting soft. Put him on the phone now. And your little tape. Don't think I forgot. It'll be all over ESPN before sunrise."

I was quiet for a moment. In theory, I really wanted to be there for my boy. Jaboe was giving me one last shot to save myself. Was I really a hero? Or would I live to regret not giving in to pressure?

"I don't think you're gonna do that."

"What? You high down there or something? 'Cause you talking like you out your mind."

"Before you dropped out of school I used to hang at your crib a lot."

"Yeah, so. What's that gotta do with anything?"

"So just as quick you can release this so-called tape you got on me, I'll have the po-po at your house searching your stuff. And I still know a few of your enemies that would love to know where you hang out. You think it's cool for you to threaten me and my friends?"

"Listen up and listen good. Damarius works for me; he owes me. You gon' sit here and stick up for him? I ain't got time for you to make it through four years of college and maybe make it in the pros. You might have an accident and find your legs broken before you even make it to Tech next season."

For a moment he caught me off guard when he knew my life's plans. But then again, who in the state didn't know where I had chosen to go? So I took a deep breath. Took another moment to think and swallowed hard.

"See. Now you're thinking. You better think before you decide to do this."

"Do what?"

"Go against me."

"You're not gonna have to wait too long to get your money back."

"Where you gonna get it from? Your daddy? I hear his dealership's not doing too well."

Jaboe was good. He knew exactly what to do to get a brother back down. What the heck was he talking about my dad's dealership not doing good? Now he sounded like the one who was smoking crack. I'm sure my dad had at least five grand around even if his cars weren't moving off the lot.

"Look, man. I want my money in five days."

"Wait, wait. I'm not getting it from my dad. We need a little more time."

"A little bit more time? No. I want my merchandise tomorrow, and I want my money in four days."

"You'll get your merchandise when we get back home."

"Where are y'all?"

"Again, you'll get your merchandise as soon as we get back in Augusta. I think D probably got some money for you too."

"Yeah. He better. He made some drops today. He owes me big."

"Give us until the end of the month. If you don't get it then, we will owe you."

"Oh. Both of you owe me now. May thirtieth at twelve AM. Y'all got thirty days. You got balls, Perry. I see why you can handle yourself on the field like that."

The next thing I knew the cell phone went silent. Cole, Jordan and Damarius were all in my face trying to see what happened.

"We got thirty days to give him money. We got four days to

give him the rest of this stuff you were going to sell down here."

"You the man, boy," Damarius said and gave me five.

Truth be told, I was real nervous most of the time I was on the phone with that thug. Settling into committing to do what I had to, the Lord gave me the courage to stand my ground. It was one of my proudest moments.

The next Saturday I was on the campus of Paine College with some of my mother's sorority sisters. They sponsored the Beautillion program to refine gentlemen. We had several polishing workshops and after months of training and preparation, it would end with a ball. Basically, it was the equivalent to the Debutante cotillion. Boy did I hate having to leave Panama City. I had been strong and had made sure my partners had some sense as well, but now I had to be at this Beautillion meeting.

I would be so happy when the actual ceremony was over. I'd missed a few sessions due to traveling. Having to deal with all the stuff with the accident. This was my first session in a while.

The brothers of the fraternity were conducting this session on teenage drug and alcohol abuse. When I came into the room I got a lot of cheers. I didn't want anyone to feel pity for me, but they knew that I had survived the whole ordeal of losing a friend.

"Hello, gentlemen. I'm Scooter Paine, a member of Iota Phi Theta Fraternity. Let me give you a little background on my fraternity. We were founded in September, 1963, in Baltimore, Maryland, during the struggles of the civil rights movement. Our colors, brown and gold, represent the natural aspects of our brotherhood. Together we work hard and proud."

I had to admit I didn't know a whole lot about the group,

but I really appreciated what they stood for. I didn't know if I'd have time to pledge when I went to Tech, but the other thing about being a Beau was that we'd get to interact with the other Greek organizations that were out there.

"I'm Brother Post. And today we're gonna talk about teen drinking and substance abuse. I don't wanna really dig into any specific experiences you've had, unless you guys wanna share. We're gonna target the subject in a general way."

It was weird getting looks from everybody. It was no secret what had caused the major auto accident that took place in our city. Even though I knew alcohol wasn't good for teens, it was nice to hear more facts about why this stuff should be left alone.

Mr. Paine said, "Can any of you guys give some reasons why you should say no to drugs?"

One boy raised his hand and said, "Because your parents say you shouldn't."

People laughed. I knew this wasn't a laughing matter. I remembered the beginning of the year for me when I felt like I was gonna die, and then witnessing what it did to Damarius.

I blurted out, "The laughing needs to stop. Alcohol is a drug and it can become addictive. It can make you do crazy things. It can mess up your mind. And when you are under its influence, it leads to bad decisions."

They went on to tell us that alcohol makes a person dangerous behind the wheel. A person who is under the influence is also more likely to have unprotected sex.

"Hey you guys may think I'm tough and I know my limits," Mr. Post said. "Truth is, once you're into it you don't even realize when you've crossed over into the danger zone."

Mr. Paine said, "Here's some other facts. Alcohol can destroy your health. The more you drink the more you hurt yourself. Alcohol poisoning occurs when you drink too much.

The level of alcohol in your blood causes blood pressure to go up, and can cause seizures or vomiting."

Now I realized what had happened to me. I had had too much alcohol in my body.

"I heard of cirrhosis of the liver," Jordan piped up.

"And what do you know about it?" Mr. Paine asked.

"It stops your liver from functioning the way that it should, like being able to clean up the poisons in your body."

"That's correct. And it can also lead to stomach ulcers. And that may lead to internal bleeding."

"Can't drinking too much alcohol give you bad breath? Cause my Uncle Phil's breath stinks all the time and he always have a bottle in his hand." Everybody laughed again.

"No. He's serious, guys. Alcohol can make you gain weight. It can make you feel dizzy, clumsy. It can slur your speech. Your skin can break out. And it causes bad breath.

"Let me give you guys some other statistics," Mr. Post said. "According to the National Institute of Alcohol Abuse, adolescents who drink before age fifteen are more likely to depend on alcohol than people who start drinking at age twenty-one.

"And in the U.S., it is estimated over three million teenagers are alcoholics," Mr. Paine said. "And you know what gets me the most is the reason we're trying to make you understand today that this is a big deal. In people between the ages of fifteen and twenty-four are alcohol-related car accidents, homicide, and suicide. Do y'all understand what I'm saying here? That means a car crash—or somebody killing themselves because of what someone did to them—were because of drinking." People looked over at me. "Y'all know what I'm talking 'bout," Mr. Paine said. "Anybody wanna share?"

I didn't wanna say anything. Everyone knew what had happened and why. But maybe this was why I went through it—to make sure everybody got it.

So I stood and said, "I'm still hurting from what alcohol did to the life of one of my friends. Well, actually all of my closest friends. I wasn't in the car that night but I saw it. I wish it had never happened, but it did—and alcohol was the reason. New Year's Eve, I was pressured to drink a little and I didn't have the willpower to say no. And everything we talked about today hit home in so many ways. I haven't touched an illegal substance but I've witnessed what it can do to people in my life. I'm trying to get hooked on something now myself. I'm trying to get high and drunk off the Word of God."

"Whew. Amen, brother," Mr. Paine said.

"I don't know. Just take it from me that having God in your life is better than any high."

Everyone came up one at a time to give me fives and pat me on the back. I appreciated every single gesture. More than any of that I hoped they understood that the effects of substance abuse and alcohol are not just something we went through. This was something that we needed to remember for the rest of our lives. Whether you're an adult or a teenager, too much of anything bad can kill you.

And as we walked out of that session as stronger young men I felt deep down that most of us would be able to apply positive pressure if ever faced with situations where people wanted us to drink. I couldn't be sure that we all would do the right thing all the time, but at least I knew we had a better chance.

The next weekend was Savoy's prom. And when I asked my dad could we get another limo, he told me that he was trying to watch the dealership's dollars and to take a town car. I wanted to ask him if everything was all right. It reminded me of what Jaboe said when I was on vacation—that they were going through tough times. But I just shrugged it off and left his problems up to him. Some things weren't meant for me to be worried about.

As I stepped inside the luxury vehicle wearing a black tux with red accessories, I prayed. *Lord, I'm really enjoying my time with my father. He said he's straight with me. He's talking cool to me. And I just wanna bless him. And bless his company. Also Lord, bless this night for Savoy. I know I haven't been a good boyfriend so let the night go smoothly and don't let me ruin it. In Jesus' name I pray. Amen.*

When I arrived at her house I sat in her driveway for about five minutes. I'd gotten there early and I needed that extra time to reflect about why I felt so awful. Many times over I'd talked to Damarius and Cole, until I practically got on their nerves, about being with one girl. And all those times I didn't understand what they were trying to tell me.

It was something inside of them that made them unsatisfied with just one girl. Now I knew how they felt. I'd been in love with Tori since I was in the tenth grade. And now that I'd been with her, which was something that I'd wanted for so long, Savoy wouldn't have my whole heart because I'd been with another girl.

When I first met Savoy, she told me how the white boys treated her better than the black guys did. I'd assured her that I would never hurt her. But if she knew what had gone on with my ex, she'd be crushed. I was no better than any other trifling guy she had described. But at least I could give her the prom of her life.

So I went to the door, straightened my tux, held the red, pink, and white corsage, and rang the doorbell.

Her mom said, "Ooh. Don't you look handsome! Come on in. Savoy, it's your date."

Before Savoy came downstairs, her father motioned for me to step into their living room.

"Yes, sir. How are you doing this evening?" I said, extending my hand.

He didn't shake it. He folded his arms and sternly said, "Listen. I got a teenage son your exact same age. And I know how it is when you guys wanna conquer something on prom night. I know even good kids lose their minds on this evening. I wanna let you know that curfew's midnight. I know you're driving tonight and wanna make it clear there will be no drinking. Treat my little girl with respect tonight. Saxon let it slip that he's a little ticked off that you're coming to spoil his prom."

"Spoil his prom? I don't understand."

"Saxon has always ruled the school. You know what I mean. I know you're the big dog over at Laney and with you coming tonight, you'll be the main attraction. Now don't let any girls lure you away from my daughter. We understand each other?"

"Sir, I have the utmost respect for your daughter."

"Good," he said, and slapped me on the back real hard. I flew a couple of steps forward.

I completely stopped in my tracks when I saw the gorgeous girl before me. Savoy's long hair was nicely swept into a beautiful French roll. The tight red dress she had on fit her body so well. At this moment I felt like a hungry dog. I gently reached over and kissed her on the cheek.

I said, "You look beautiful." She beamed with pride.

Her grandmother was there, and a few other relatives. They took bundles of pictures. After she placed the corsage on her hand, we were done with the family paparazzi and were able to take off.

"So where's your brother?" I asked, not really wanting to know.

"You just missed him. He thinks he's a stud with him going with a girl from college."

"Oh really? Well he won't have the best looking girl there," I said, looking over at her.

"Stop it before I burst. You're making me feel so special. And we never talked about your prom. How was it?"

"Nothing to talk about. When I was at mine I was looking forward to taking you to yours."

"Perry, you're just saying all the right things. Is Tori feeling better? I mean I can't imagine how it feels to lose your best friend. But then I sorta can when Ellis pulled that stunt trying to come on to you. Ever since then we've been at odds. I never thought we would fall out over a guy, but we haven't spoken since."

I didn't wanna tell her that her friend was trifling, and that she didn't need to feel bad about not hanging out with that girl. I didn't wanna make her feel worse. And I actually hated that I was the reason Ellis had shown her true colors.

"I mean a best friend is supposed to be someone you put your whole trust into. Someone who may have problems themselves but will find a way to help you out. They won't intentionally let you down. And they won't lie to your face."

As she went on and on I was feeling smaller and smaller. I was her boyfriend and Tori was my ex. I'd gotten myself in such a mess.

When we pulled into the hotel parking lot where the prom was supposed to be, I leaned over and kissed her. I needed to clear her mind of all negative thinking. Tonight was about her. But when we walked inside and everybody started whispering about me, I felt uncomfortable.

"So you know you're the man tonight, right?" she said.

"I don't know why. I mean, your brother's cool in my book. We're just two senior guys trying to do our thing."

"Well, everybody loves Sax. He's such a leader and he makes everybody feel cool. But you're a gentleman. You hold the door for strangers. He would close the door in their faces or wait till they did it for him. My brother drives me crazy sometimes."

Just as she said that we heard a loud voice say, "Gather around people. I am now at the prom; it can now begin."

When I turned around I saw it was Saxon, motioning for an audience to gather around. The girl on his arm was a cutie.

"Yeah. She's cute, huh?" Savoy said, as she noticed I was checking out the girl.

"She all right."

"You liar!" she said as she hit me in the side. "That's Brandy Wells. She used to go here last year. Now she's a freshman at South Carolina State. They said she'd be homecoming queen every year, but there you gotta be a senior, so as a freshman she didn't qualify."

Nobody was dancing—and this was prom! These country people didn't know how to do it like us Augusta folks. So I said to Savoy, "Let's get this party started. Can I have this dance?"

When the two of us got on the floor and started jamming to the slow song, it didn't take long for people to join us.

The next thing I knew Sax got all in my face and started talking trash. It didn't take me long to figure out he was drunk.

"Come on, man. Step aside."

"No, dog. This is my house; I run the show. No dancing first on the floor and all that. Move out my way. You ain't all that."

Then he pushed. It took everything I had inside to keep from waxing his butt. But his sister came to my rescue and said, "Saxon, why you gotta mess up the prom by drinking? Everybody knows who you are. Nobody's trying to take your status away. Just because people are intrigued with Perry you don't have to get jealous."

When he slapped his hand across her face, I lost it. That

was his sister and he didn't need to hit her. I went up and grabbed his shirt by the collar. Looking him up and down, I realized I was a little bigger and tougher than he was.

"Nobody's trying to make you look like a fool, Saxon. You're doing it all to yourself. You should've been at the session we had last week. That was definitely one you shouldn't have missed. Go clean yourself up before you get expelled."

I went over to Savoy and held her close while she let out a few tears. "My brother has been drunk a lot lately. It's killing me. I don't understand what he's doing. Why can't he be perfect like you?"

Quickly I said, as I tilted her chin up to my face, "I'm not perfect. You don't know how hard it is trying to maintain your popularity, fearing somebody might steal your thunder."

I got up and danced with Savoy. And as I rocked her back and forth in my arms I felt right. I wanted to be her knight in shining armor. I wanted her to be safe. I wanted her to be the envy of the ball.

She looked at me and said, "You are the best." Then we shared another special kiss. I realized that even though I was far from perfect, it was okay to relax a bit and start enjoying life's moments.

~ 14 ~

Scaring Us All

It was Mother's Day weekend and Payton was home. My parents had been getting along great after several weeks of constant arguments. As I came downstairs, though, I heard shouting.

My mom sounded defensive, "This is Mother's Day weekend. Why should I have to spend it driving to Conyers? My daughter's home and I wanna spend it with her. You invited your mother down here to share this day with her but she refused. Why are you trying to ruin my plans?"

"What do you have against my mother?" my dad asked.

"Nothing. It's just when I get the hint something weird is going on with her or I bring up her constant need for money, all of a sudden you get defensive, Perry."

My mom didn't call my father "Perry" often. So when I heard her call him by his first name, I knew she was heated. And it was true how defensive he was about his mother. I didn't know that grandma had been calling asking for money lately. Maybe I was the only one who knew the truth about what was really going on with her.

I was torn whether to speak up or keep quiet. Then I remembered that I promised grandma I wouldn't say a word. I just hoped my folks would work it out. Payton came down the stairs behind me and pushed me into the room with my parents.

"Okay, Mom and Dad. I didn't come all the way down home to hear y'all yelling. Can't we figure this out as a family?"

"See, honey, look. You got Payton all upset."

"No, Dad. Don't throw me into this. It's Mother's Day. We want our mom to be happy just like you want your mom to be happy. And I think we can accomplish all of that. Mom, we don't wanna leave you here while we go see her. We'll all be up bright and early to go to seven o'clock service. That way when service is over, we can drive on up to Conyers and still be back here to have dinner."

"His mom don't wanna see me. She just wants to see you guys. If that's how you feel, Payton, then y'all can go up there yourselves."

My mom tried to walk past me to go to her room but I wouldn't let her by. I put my arms around her and squeezed her tight. "Mom, we love you. Payton's right. Let's just go up there. Grandma's got way more issues—I mean, grandma . . . Let's just go see her."

"Son, what are you saying? You talked to my mom?"

"No. I was just saying."

I realized I was saying too much. Grandma and I had talked about a lot more than me cutting her grass.

"My mom won't expect to see us long. She wasn't expecting us to come at all."

"Yeah, right. That's just her ploy to get sympathy. Everybody wants me to go? Fine. I'll go," my mom huffed.

Thankfully my mom gave in and after church we were headed to my grandmother's crib. My parents still had a little battle going on. Even though I was uneasy with the tension I couldn't fix all the world's problems.

So I took advantage of the fact that my sister was sitting

beside me. Last time she and I talked we both had issues about not being able to keep our temptations under control. I didn't wanna open up a can of worms 'cause I knew if I asked her what was going on in her life she would ask me the same.

I certainly didn't wanna tell her that I was a virgin no more, but I really wanted to ask about her and Tad. Dang, I hated being torn. I was eighteen. It was time for me to take a stand and make my own decisions.

"Why you so fidgety over there?" Payton asked me. She leaned over and whispered, "You ain't smoking no weed, are you?"

"No, girl. Why you say that?"

"'Cause look at your lips. Right around the middle of your lips they're getting dark. I see it all the time in college. I know what I'm talking about."

"My lips just changing colors. I don't do none of that stuff."

I thought, *That's your seventy-five-year-old grandmother you're about to check out in a few. Not me.* But of course I kept quiet about that little detail.

"What's up with you and your boy?"

"I don't even wanna go there. I might've scared him away."

"What you mean?"

"I mean pushing him into something he wasn't ready to do. I might have lost him for good."

My sister looked real sad. She stared out the window. I gently lifted her hand and squeezed it. She looked over at me and smiled.

"I'll be all right."

"I hope so."

When we pulled up to grandma's house, her lawn looked a mess. My dad started fussing. "I don't know what she been doing with that money I been sending her. She said that Mr. Jeffrey been coming every week to take care of her lawn. It looks like nobody touched this grass in a month!"

"Yeah, and I bet she don't have new pots either. I bet she don't have the flat-screen she was dying to have and all that other stuff she pleaded for you to get her. The way we gotta watch our funds now and your mom calling for all this and that nonsense, I know she's doing something else with it. I believe she got a boyfriend she's taking care of."

"Mom!" Payton said from the backseat.

"You know what, Payton, I'm not even gonna fuss with your mom about this. Let's just go in the house," my dad said.

Dad rang the doorbell about eight times. "You didn't even call her to let her know we were coming?" my mom said with an attitude.

"No, I wanted to surprise her. Plus, the way you were acting I wasn't sure we were coming."

I started fearing grandma wasn't doing okay so I began pounding on the door. "Boy, what's wrong with you?" my dad asked.

"She might be upstairs or way in the back. You know it's Sunday so she probably got the gospel music blasting and she might not be able to hear. Grandma! Grandma!" I shouted.

"Hey y'all!" Grandma greeted us as she opened the door. Her eyes started fluttering towards the back of her head, and out of her mouth came a trail of smoke.

"Oh, my gosh, Grandma!" Payton yelled out. "That's a joint in your hand!"

"Oh, baby. That's just my medicine."

"Mom, what you talking about medicine?"

"Oh, hush now. Just come on in." The smoke was so thick in her house it actually made us cough. "Payton, baby. I used to smoke cigarettes when I was your age. And now I got this here old lung cancer, and breast cancer, and now this stuff just hurt. You so pretty girl. Don't you dare use none of that stuff. Them cigarettes is addictive."

"Grandma, what you talking 'bout cancer? Dad!" shouted Payton.

"Mom, what are you saying?"

"Oh, my sweet little grandson. You ain't said nothing? Bless your heart. Come here and give me a hug."

"What she talking about, Perry?" my dad asked coldly.

"Ooh, my chest hurt. I gotta sit down."

I explained to my parents about how a few months back I caught Grandma smoking a joint to fight off the pain of her cancer. My dad looked like he could choke me for keeping something like this from him. My mom just hugged me. I felt so bad.

Suddenly my grandma collapsed on the floor. My sister called the paramedics but they seemed to take forever to get there. *What had I done by keeping this to myself?* I thought guiltily. We were all terrified. Even my mother. We all prayed that we didn't lose my grandmother.

We spent the rest of Mother's Day in the hospital, but no one minded. Even my mom and sister stayed there until we knew something. My father didn't wanna speak to me. I knew I let him down but I thought I was doing the right thing.

As we waited for some kind of answer from the doctor, I walked away to the hospital chapel. Immediately I fell to my knees on the prayer pillow.

I said, "Lord, I know I wasn't the one who made my grandmother take drugs to make herself feel better. And for some reason I feel like crap. I'm sorry. I didn't know if I should say that to you but I mean it. I really feel like crap. I knew she was using marijuana and didn't tell anybody. You know that I didn't realize it was so serious, but does that excuse me? I know I'm no doctor. Please, be with her now. Help her get well. Please."

I felt a hand touching my shoulder. I couldn't look up. I didn't want anybody to see the tears on my face. But I knew that touch belonged to my father.

"Son, I'm sorry I came down on you, making you think it was your fault. Mom just came out of it. She's conscious and the doctor explained everything. It looks like a couple of her friends that have cancer hooked her up with this home remedy. They hooked her up with a guy who's been bringing the stash by. She said she'd sworn you to keep it to yourself 'cause she knew what she was doing. But it looks like it spiraled out of control."

"Dad, I'm sorry. I should've told you."

"I know, son. But I'm not mad at you for keeping your promise to your grandma. I am disappointed that you knew about something so life-threatening as cancer, and you didn't follow up on her and keep checking with her. Make sure she's okay. But we're all learning."

My dad and I embraced. Even though he'd let me off the hook I was still down on myself. He made a great point. And if my grandmother's confession to me was a cry for help, then I should've told my family.

"I just feel so bad, Dad," I said, letting out some tears.

"Son, don't do this to yourself. Don't put so much pressure on yourself. Truth be told, I should've been in touch with my mom more. I just kept giving her what she wanted to get her off my back. Your mom told me to dig deeper into the story but I was a knucklehead and didn't listen. Like I said earlier, we're all learning."

We walked back to my grandmother's room and held her hand as she rested. My parents were hugged up. My sister had her head in our grandmother's lap. We all were breathing a little easier knowing that she was okay for now.

That Wednesday I had to go to a Beautillion meeting. The men of Alpha Phi Alpha, the fraternity founded in 1906, were the leaders of our session on peer pressure. None of us wanted to talk at first but then Saxon came in late and was happy to share.

"It's something we all cave into. You either do what the in-crowd says to do or you might as well stay home."

"What if what the in-crowd tells you to do is dangerous?" the leader of the discussion said.

Saxon shrugged his shoulders. "Then you gotta do what I do."

"Why?"

"So you won't ever let anyone know you're afraid."

"That's a good strategy you're using there, Mr. Lee."

"I'm Mr. Lee as well," the leader replied.

"Oh, okay then partner," Saxon said, as went up to the front and shook the man's hand.

"But it's also a dumb reason, son," our leader said. "You're the strong one. Use your peer pressure for something positive. Would a true Beau, a true gentleman, a true man show us strength not by leading the crowd to do whatever he wants to do but by using his influence to do the right thing because it's the better decision?"

We did a lot of role-playing exercises where the pressure was on to drink. Saxon and I were teamed up, and he got to be the friend who wanted to act stupid. And I had to be the one who went against the grain.

"Aw, come on man. Have a drink with me."

"No, partner. I'm straight."

"Please, man. You ain't got it going on. But if you hit this you'll be feeling right."

Saxon was acting his role so stupid and silly that people were laughing through the whole scene. They weren't even getting the point that the pressure was real sometimes. It was easy to do what your friends wanted.

"Here, here. Try this," he said as if he was putting an imaginary joint in my face.

"No, man. I said I'm straight."

"Oh, so it's like that. You gonna turn down your friend?"

"Why you can't respect my decision that I don't want that stuff to fry my brain? Why you just can't be cool with knowing that I want to keep all my faculties intact? I wouldn't wanna go to the prom and make a fool of myself on the dance floor."

All of a sudden Saxon pushed me. Again it was like déjà-vu—this skit was becoming really real to me. Saxon and I hadn't talked since that crazy night he was acting stupid. The alcohol made him trip. He needed to understand that it wasn't cool with me then and it wasn't cool with me now. So I pushed him back and punched him in the face a couple of times until his nose got real bloody.

"Hey, Perry. You gonna finish the skit or what?" Saxon said, as he saw me shake my head. I had been daydreaming. "You're supposed to tell me why I don't need this stuff," he leaned over and whispered.

"You know why. It makes you do silly things and I'm just not down with it." I walked away and went to my seat, leaving him standing there looking crazy.

The mind plays crazy tricks on you sometimes. I had to keep my thoughts in check.

"I liked that, Mr. Skky. Sometimes you have to walk away from your pressure. It's not about being the cool one. It's about being the smart one. When you're taking a chance and doing what's right you're always cool. And if you got a cool platform like some of you got in here, then folks might like to follow you for what you stand for. Remember positive peer pressure."

As we left, Saxon laughed under his breath. I knew he wasn't going to pick up a thing from that workshop. And that makes the presenters and the rest of us that learned something a little lame. I just hated that people sometimes didn't listen. But what could I do?

The last two weeks of May were extra crazy. I had to go to debutante practice every night. I remembered when my sister was in the Links' version of the male Beautillion. I had no idea of all the practice required to perform the waltz.

I knew Tori was a junior deb. She kept talking about it and she kept asking me if I was escorting that girl from Aiken. I couldn't just back out of my commitment. I don't know how I was going to juggle having both of them at this event, with each girl thinking I was committed to her alone.

Thankfully junior debs were only hostesses. They didn't require dates. So I was able to mask my involvement with Savoy till showtime.

The evening started out picture-perfect. The senior girls had on their white satin gowns. We were decked out in our white tuxes with tails. Saxon was a big jerk for escorting Savoy's ex-best friend. He knew his sister was through with the girl. Clearly he didn't care about her feelings.

Jordan was there too, escorting Amandi. They were an odd couple but he just wanted to be in the mix. I was happy though 'cause it kept her away from me. Though I'd got a peek at some of the girls, I didn't get to actually see Savoy until I escorted her mother to the end of the stage while we waited for Savoy and her father to walk toward us.

Savoy had such confidence. While I watched other girls shake and fret to strut their stuff, she didn't hold back anything. And I couldn't help but smile. As the announcers read all of her accomplishments, I desperately wanted to take her from her daddy's arms and dance slow all night long.

When we finally got a chance to present the choreographed dance number to the audience, I said to Savoy, "Hello pretty lady."

"I'm so glad you're my partner," she said. "My brother told me to ask somebody else. I just think he didn't want you to steal the show from him again. But every girl in here wishes she was dancing with you, anyway."

"Yeah, right. And you don't think every guy in here doesn't wish you were his date? You're the debutante queen."

I had to admit that the dance was actually cool. It had better be with all the rehearsing that we'd put into it. Doing the figure eight, learning the two-step and cha-cha-cha was not easy. It was all synchronized so nicely tonight. Forty couples jammed. We got a standing ovation when it was over. Next, the girls had to dance with their fathers and the guys danced with their mothers. Then we got to waltz with our dates and the parents danced.

"What are you thinking about?" Savoy asked me, as she rubbed her hand up and down my side.

"I'm thinking you're trying to get us both in trouble here."

"Would that be so bad?"

I couldn't even answer her question. And thankfully all the debutantes were called to the stage to sing their debutante hymn. I opened up the program and read along. As the words sorta moved me, it was really freaky to know that we were about done with high school. I was now reflecting, wishing time would slow up a bit. Everything that was happening, I didn't want it to just go by without it meaning something to me.

"I'm a budding rose, blooming and blossoming into a creation. I'm at the point of my life where I want to be, and where God needs me to be. I'm a debutante. And I'm proud to be one."

Seeing them all hug each other I knew I had to make this night special. And as the crowd dispersed I turned around and saw Tori standing straight in front of me.

"Okay, this lovey-dovey thing you got going on with Savoy needs to end right now."

Her mom and dad looked at me like I was supposed to handle that. And I was just caught off guard because I couldn't believe that Tori came to me like that. I tried pulling her to the side, but she wouldn't move.

"What's the problem?"

"You are my boyfriend and I've been watching you all night from the door as I handed out programs, being somebody's else date. Before the night is over you need to dance with me."

"Tori, you're acting crazy. This isn't the time or place where you should be coming into my face like that," I said, annoyed.

She was tripping! But what could I expect? I hadn't done anything to let her know that I was her man. And when I saw Savoy with her hand on her hip with Ellis by her side, I knew I was in deep trouble.

"So, is this Tori? Is this your ex-girlfriend? Why is she telling everybody that you guys are still a hot item?"

I couldn't believe I was in the middle of a big crowd of debutantes, parents, friends, grandparents, and all the other spectators, speechless.

"Oh, you're gonna tell her?" Tori said from the side. "I'm not his ex-girlfriend, Savoy."

"He told me he was just comforting you when you were bruised and sad about your girlfriend. I knew y'all was hanging out as friends but nothing more."

"See, ma, you kept saying that that boy was a goody-two-shoes," Saxon said from behind Savoy and Ellis. "He's a player like me. I can't even give you five though dog 'cause you played my sister."

I walked up to Savoy and said, "Look. I really do need to explain some things. I don't wanna deal with it here. Can we go somewhere and talk?" I asked as I took her hand.

Snatching it away she said, "We don't need to talk about anything ever. I gave you an out on our relationship. You didn't take it and now I'm looking like a fool. I was just telling my mom how lucky I was to be your girl," Savoy was telling me as she lifted the hem of her dress and stomped off.

I turned around and looked at Tori and could only shake my head. I went over to Savoy's father and said, "Sir, I'm sorry. I didn't mean this to cause a scene."

"Keep your weak apologies to yourself, bro." Saxon told me.

"Son, hush," his father told him.

I tried to ease through the crowd but it was so packed I had to utter every second, "Excuse me; can I get through?"

"Girls need a hot man on their arm like you, baby. I don't care if I'm number two, three, four, five or six. I hear you about to make big paper. I'm a little older than you but I can wait," one of the ladies I was trying to pass by said. As I stood there gritting my teeth, she finally let me pass.

Then I felt Tori pulling on my back. "Wait! You can't leave me. You took everything I had. You told me you loved me. If you couldn't break up with her I had to break up with her for you. I lost my best friend, Perry. You know what that did to me. I can't lose you too."

She fell to the ground. Thankfully her mother came through the crowd and told me to go on, and she had her. I knew juggling the two of them was gonna blow up in my face eventually. I just had no idea how big of an explosion it was gonna be.

It was now clear which girl I definitely wanted to be with. And Savoy was never going to speak to me again. All I felt was empathy for Tori. Her over-the-top actions were making everybody at the ball worried. As I went to get my keys, I could only pray she'd get it together. As I replayed her frantic antics in my mind, she was scaring us all.

~ 15 ~

Coming Out Strong

A fist hit me square in the mouth as I opened the Civic Center door to exit the cotillion. It caught me so off-guard that I immediately fell to the ground. Tasting the salty blood in my mouth, I was furious. What the heck was going on?

I couldn't rise up quickly to defend myself 'cause I was yanked by two dudes, one grabbing my left arm and one grabbing my right. Then I looked up and saw Jaboe. As he took one of his hands and placed it tightly around my throat, he quickly pulled out a knife.

"Where's my money, pretty boy?"

"Jaboe this ain't the end of the month. Plus, I know you see I'm all dressed up. You better watch what you do because there's a lot of people inside," I said in a voice I didn't even recognize. Because he held my throat so tight my pitch was off.

"Maybe it is a good idea if I kill you here. At least you know somebody will find you right away. You're not asking the questions, I am. Now where's my money?"

"Damarius said he gave you a thousand dollas already. Now all we owe you is four grand. Come on, man. I can't breathe."

Jaboe just looked at me and kept on applying more pressure. I couldn't even use my legs as a defense 'cause the way he had my neck, my legs weren't loose. I let out a grunt and he let my neck go.

"You think that hurt? Wait until you see what happens if I don't get my money."

"You said we had till the end of the month."

"I changed my mind," Jaboe leaned over and said coldly. "Instead of having two more weeks, you got one. Next Saturday night I want my money and extra if you don't have my loot."

As soon as I looked up they were gone. This had clearly been one of the worst days I remembered having in a long time. But what was I gonna do, pout about it? Be a wimp? What the heck would that solve?

Before I reached my car Jordan jogged over to me. "Hey Perry! Wait up."

My back was turned so he didn't see my busted lip. When I slowly turned around he saw all the blood on my white tailored shirt.

"Dang man! I heard Savoy went off on you but did her dad punch you or something?"

"No. It's much worse than that, partner. I'm headed over to Damarius's house now."

"You got your keys? Can you roll out? You gotta stay? What?"

"No, my keys in my pocket."

"What's going on? Talk to me. It's that drug dealer cat, ain't it?" Jordan asked, in a sincere tone.

"Yeah. He ain't playing either. We gotta get his money."

As soon as I cranked up my car I turned down my radio and called Cole. "Hello? Cole, man. What you doing?"

"Watching the NBA playoffs. What's going on?"

"Look, I know the Mavericks your team and all but I need you to meet me over at Damarius's crib. We got a big situation."

"I'm there."

I really respected Cole. He was a good buddy. Anything you asked of him he was there for you. I would've given him more information about what I'd be expecting if Jaboe's buddies were over D's house roughing him up. But, I didn't get the chance because Cole hung up on me and I knew he was grabbing his keys to meet me.

I frantically dialed Damarius's line three times and each time the phone was busy. Surely Jaboe wouldn't take things too far before he got his dough.

I just prayed. *Lord. I'm coming to you now because I'm feeling pressure. But I know even though I'm worried for my boy, you don't want me to stress at all. I don't know what kind of plan we can put together to get four grand in a week. And it doesn't even seem fair that I come to you and ask you to help us square things with the drug dealer. But we need you. Please, Lord.*

I turned my radio back on and switched from my favorite hip-hop station to a CD with some inspirational tunes. My dad was a big John P. Keith fan and one of his old CDs was playing in my car. The song was entitled "Stand." And just like the words in it, I was committed to standing for holiness. Standing for righteousness. And standing up for truth.

I didn't know what kind of encounter I was getting ready for. And I honestly worried that Jordan was right behind me and Cole was on his way, because if anything crazy was going down, I didn't want anybody else getting hurt. But when I saw Jaboe's familiar ride glide by us from Damarius's neighborhood, I sped up. I hoped we weren't too late. But I was relieved we had avoided a confrontation.

When I arrived at Damarius's house the front door was wide open. I told Jordan to stand guard at the front door. When I yelled out for my friend he didn't answer. The place was ransacked. When I got to his room he was crawling onto his bed. His eye on the right side was swollen shut.

"Perry. Cole's here," Jordan called out in the house.

"All right. I found D. He's back here. I need some ice, though."

Cole busted through the door and said, "What's going on? Your lip is busted and your eye is swollen. Both of y'all are looking crazy. We gotta take care of this. Y'all think of something. Look at him."

"I'm all right," Damarius whispered.

Seeing him tore up I started to worry about Jaboe's demands. Frustration was starting to sink in because we couldn't come up with a plan that made sense.

Then Jordan said, "Y'all are ballplayers. Y'all got skills. All the little kids worship y'all. Let's pull a fundraiser."

"In a week? How we gonna pull that off?" Damarius said, as he held the ice to his wounded eye.

"We can't be negative. We just gotta think harder. And maybe it's gonna take more than the four of us to get it together. I gotta call my dad."

"You ain't the only one," Damarius said. "I gotta call my pops too."

I didn't know that his parents were separated again. His dad was living in a trailer on the other side of town. Funny thing was his mom was hanging out over there. Damarius explained to us that his parents were getting along better apart than together.

When both of our dads arrived I was glad that they didn't give us any grief. The parental support they both gave us was amazing. As we straightened up, my dad told us that he was a member of the Aquinas Club. He would go around to different businesses and ask them to donate what they could.

Damarius's old man said, "Look, guys. Messing with Jaboe ain't no joke. Son, I wish you would've came to me and let me know how deep you were in this thing. You must've forgot I was in it like that too. As you can see, messing with another man's drugs can get you into trouble in a lot of ways." We couldn't call the cops because an illegal activity had got us into this in the first place.

But a week later by God's grace we'd organized a football clinic for two hundred fifty-three boys in Augusta who dreamed of being ballplayers. During the event Jaboe and his crew pulled up by the concession stand. I knew they weren't here to buy anything. My dad saw them and waved an envelope towards Jaboe. When he started walking toward him I did the same. It wasn't my dad's battle to fight.

"So you asked your dad for the money anyway," Jaboe said in a smart way. "I thought you were broke, Mr. Skky."

"Here. Just take your money. I want you to leave my son and his friends alone for good. Is that clear?"

"Yes, sir. I'm a big fan of your son's. I wouldn't dream of hurting him or his friends. Look like all of it's here," Jaboe said as he looked in the envelope. "I'm just a thing of the past." As soon as he turned around three cops were standing behind him. "Excuse me, officers. I was just leaving."

The one in the middle said, "We know your game, son. We trust your business is done here."

"I don't want no trouble with the po-po."

The look the officer gave me was stern. Behind his eyes I could tell that he was telling me, "You got off lucky this time." The officer came up to me and said, "When hanging with the wrong crowd, you can be pressured to do the wrong thing. Be smarter than that. Take your skills and get away from this life."

I shook his hand and said, "I got you, sir."

When all the kids were gone, I thanked my dad properly. He told me he'd always be there for me and I truly believed that. Damarius wouldn't let me leave without doing the same thing. He didn't owe me anything for this. I should've stood up for him a long time ago. But you can't look back in life. You can only look forward.

But I was glad I followed the Holy Spirit to call on God when I needed help. 'Cause only then did everything work out okay.

The next day after church my mom asked me what I wanted for dinner.

I said, "I don't know, Mom. I'm really not that hungry. Can I talk to you for a second?"

"Sure, baby. Sit down. What's going on?"

"I really messed up. Broke some girls' hearts. And I wasn't even trying to do it. I didn't wanna be like that. I remembered when Payton was all sad when Dakari did her wrong. And I just never wanted that to be my story but I couldn't help it. I fell hard for two girls and it all blew up in my face."

"Well you should've been honest about it, son."

"Mom, you're a woman. Isn't there anything I can do to make things right?"

"Have you apologized?"

"I tried but they weren't trying to hear that."

"What happened?"

I explained to my mother how close Tori and I got at the end of the funeral. And how I didn't break things off with Savoy and how both girls thought I was exclusively theirs. And I told her about the cotillion. She rubbed her brow. I knew I'd let her down. I know that's not how she raised me.

So I asked again. "Mom, what can I do?"

"The biggest thing now, son, is time. Girls need a chance to heal. I'm seriously concerned about Tori. I know it's not our problem but we need to pray for her. I don't like hearing how you said she responded in public like that. It sounds like she's not the right girl for you."

"Yeah. She overreacted, right?"

"Well, hon. Neither of us are in her mind, in her heart, or walking in her shoes. I'm not gonna go there. She thought y'all had something special. She snapped when she saw you with someone else. That's why you gotta be careful where you lay."

I couldn't believe that my mom came right out and said that to me. But that's why I loved her so. I was heading off to college and there was no need to sugarcoat things anymore. Whether or not she approved of the fact that I was sexually active, it was a reality that I needed to deal with and, as a parent, so did she.

"I think you need to talk to both girls. Not to try and get back with either of them. You need to just speak from your heart. And even though it's gonna hurt, women know they're strong enough to take the truth, and every woman wants honesty. And if she don't then she needs to check her priorities. We're all too special to put up with bull."

Later that day I took my mom's advice and headed over to north Augusta. There was a statewide track meet and Savoy was competing. I didn't know about it since she never tooted her own horn, but Payton let me in on what Savoy was doing today. I patiently sat in the stands with a bouquet in my hands.

A couple of folks chuckled at me at first. Then word started spreading through the stadium who I was. People were asking for autographs. A few girls gave me their phone numbers. In some circles I couldn't sit in peace.

I scoured the field looking for Savoy. And when I finally found her I feasted my eyes on a lovely sight. Just watching her warm up was a treat. I realized again that I hadn't been a good boyfriend and that our relationship wasn't just about me. Here she was, a track star, and I had never actually seen her compete.

She got in position to run the one hundred. And as soon as the gun went off she took off ahead of the pack. I couldn't contain myself.

I stood and yelled, "Go, Savoy!" And within seconds she won the race.

I went down there so fast to congratulate her that I forgot the flowers. I had to jog back in the stands and get them. By the time I got back to the field, I couldn't find her. But I did bump into her parents.

"Perry Skky. What brings you down here today?" her father asked, not too overjoyed to see my face.

"I'm just trying to find your daughter, sir. I lost track of her for a second."

"Honey, I'll catch up to you in a second," her father said to Mrs. Lee.

Wasn't any need for me to back down. I already knew her dad had issues with me. He'd said a couple of things to me at the ball. Most of that night was a blur. Well really most of that night I'm trying to forget, would be a better way of putting it.

"Sir, I'm sorry that things ended up this way. I really care about your daughter and I certainly didn't mean to hurt her."

"Well you did. I don't know what you think you have to say that she would want to hear now. You need to leave, son."

"No, Dad. I want to talk to him," Savoy said, startling me as she came up to us from behind.

I turned around and was so elated to see her beautiful face. Even as the sweat poured down her body, something about her was pulling me in.

I looked back and said to her dad, "I won't be but a second, sir."

"Dad, please. Let us talk."

"Well, you need to tell him about the Beautillion, that you're not going to be able to be his escort."

"Dad, I got this. Bye."

Knowing that bit of info was like somebody hit me in the kneecaps from behind and brought me down a couple inches. No one had ever turned me down for anything. But how could I expect Savoy to stand beside me proudly when I broke her heart?

"I didn't mean for my dad to blurt that out. I was going to tell you myself."

"No, it's cool. I shouldn't be surprised. I ruined your debutante night."

"I just wanna know why. I probably would have given you sex."

"I don't think it was just that. And honestly Savoy I can't tell you why. But I had feelings for Tori that came back. We went through our grief together, we got close, one thing led to another, and as soon as it was over I regretted it. But I had already taken it too far. She automatically assumed that we were an item again. What kind of guy would I be—" I had to look away.

"To hit it and leave? Yeah that would've been kinda tacky too," Savoy said.

"I know there's no excuse for what I did. Just leave it like that. But I'm sorry. I really am. I hate that this is the first chance I had to see you run. I heard you were good but dang, girl, you might be able to beat me."

"Might be able to?" she teased.

"Okay. Maybe we can get a run in together. It'll be fun training with you. Exercise beats sex any day. I'm glad you won. These are for you." I kissed her on the cheek. "I know I let you down in a big way but I just wanna let you know, Savoy, that you'll always have a place in my heart."

"Bye, Perry," she said, trying to control her emotions.

She jogged away into the crowd, where people were waiting to celebrate her win.

Next I needed to talk to Tori. Her favorite place was Bath and Body Works. So I went there and got a cute little basket called a relaxer kit. She desperately needed to chill out. But what was I going to say to her? Hopefully the basket would help her release her anguish in a more positive way.

When I got to Tori's house I was glad to see her father's car was not in the driveway. When I rang the doorbell, he answered. I wanted to turn around and walk away. But again, that wouldn't have solved anything.

"Sir, I'm not here to come in or anything. I just wanted to talk to your daughter for a second."

"Perry Skky. You've been making my daughter shed all those tears and you expect me to allow you to speak with her? Boy, you must really think you all that."

"I don't know, sir. I just wanna try and clean up some of this."

"You're bringing her gifts and stuff, what's that all about? I hate that my daughter's all strung out over some boy. And just when I try to make sure she's over you, you come back?"

"Sir, I wanna apologize to her the right way. Let her know she can get over me. I wanna say the things that will make her feel better. Maybe she'll accept my gift and all of this will be over."

I don't know what he was about to say when he started to grit his teeth. Then he replied, "I respect that. Wait in the living room."

It took Tori about ten minutes to come out after I heard her dad tell her it was me.

As soon as she came in I said, "Good to see you."

"I thought you'd never wanna talk to me again after what I did. I'm so sorry. Will we ever be able to pick up and go on?"

"Tori, I know I should've been honest with you but I

didn't really think you would hear it. You were all sad with what was going on, and when we were together, I did feel something. I care about you a lot but I'm not in any position to be committed to anybody."

"I can't imagine you not being in a relationship with any-body."

"I guess what I'm saying to you is, I wanna be in a relation-ship with God. For me to hurt you the way I did, for me to let Savoy down, is not who I wanna be. I gotta get myself right. And I want you to do the same. You don't need me or any other guy to make you know that you got it going on. Yeah, I know your girl is gone. But you can't let all of you die too. You gotta keep living and keep being the Tori to impress me and help me grow up. All that sex, wine, and high mess you got going on, let it go. You do your thing and focus on what God has for you; you'll be weak no more. I graduate in ten days and then I leave for Tech after that. We might or might not get to see each other again, but you'll always have a part of my heart. If you need to know how to get in touch with me again, who knows. I may just be checking up on you."

Tears streamed down her face. Dang this was hard! I went over to her and handed her the basket with my right hand. And with my left, I touched her face. "I don't want you to be sad."

"A Bath and Body Works basket. Thank you."

We gave each other our last sweet kiss goodbye. And when I drove away I felt good knowing that God was gonna love her and take care of her the way I couldn't. I hadn't righted what I'd done to Tori and Savoy but at least I had taken re-sponsibility for my mistakes. And I could live with that.

The Beautillion was here. And I was actually looking for-ward to the event. The Deltas had rented a nice ballroom and I had two tables, one for my parents' friends and the other for my grandmother, Cole, Damarius, my mom, dad, Payton, and me.

Payton was actually my escort for the evening. My mom had talked her into putting on her old debutante dress. She was actually amazed that she could still fit in the old thing from two years ago. Savoy was there as Saxon's escort. We were cordial to each other. And I was a little bruised that things weren't like they used to be. But I moved on with the evening.

After the great meal of steak, shrimp, scalloped potatoes, and asparagus and the great cheesecake, it was time to announce the Beau. Before we were ready to go on stage Jordan pulled me aside.

"I just wanted to say that I really admire you."

"Boy, shut up," I said, bopping him in the head.

"No, man. Hear me out. I remember back to the beginning of the year when we had classes together. Nobody knew my name. Nobody wanted to hang out with me 'cause I was a nerd, you know. And I knew if I teamed up with you I'd be cool." He hesitated.

"Man, go ahead," I said to him. "What you trying to say?"

"I just didn't know what you, Cole, or Damarius would really mean to me. I'd never been with a group of guys who cared about each other so much that they took risks to save each other. You made alcohol and drugs unpopular. Now we want punch instead. I gave you a platform on the football field and you're doing the right thing. I made a bunch of mistakes. Maybe when you're weak I can be strong."

"That's what friendship is, right?"

"I guess what I'm trying to say, Perry, is you mean a lot to me. And I learned this year that being a true gentleman is about placing others above yourself. It's about standing up even if you have to stand alone for what's right. It's about helping your friends make right choices and treating women right. Oh, we gotta work on that." We both laughed. "But unlike most of the brothers walking around here, you cared about hurting somebody. It takes a bigger man to do the right thing. And we voted you Mr. Beau."

The rest of the guys, all except Saxon, came around me and gave me five. I had forgotten about all the forms that we had to fill out to put down someone's name on the board. I had nominated Jordan. He was so into all of those sessions he could've taught the crowd himself. And they'd given it to me. This meant I was going to have to read my speech.

Pretty soon the commentator said, "And introducing Mister Perry Skky Jr. He's the proud son of Mr. and Mrs. Perry Skky Sr. He attends Lucy Laney High School where he's an All-American football player with numerous athletic records. His sister Payton Skky has escorted him this evening. And he will be attending the Georgia Institute of Engineering and Technology in the fall. He plans to major in mechanical engineering and hopes to one day invent a new line of cars. His motto is: 'Every day I'm pushing to get better.' His favorite scripture is 'To whom much is given, much is required.' Ladies and gentlemen, our favorite football star, Mr. Perry Skky Jr."

Unlike the debs we didn't have to do a choreographed number with our escorts. Payton and I just had to do a waltz. As we danced she said, "You know, you'll always be my little brother. I'm sorta bummed out that you won't be coming to Georgia. But seeing you now, I can say that you're not just my little brother anymore. You're a young man that's handling his business. And I'm proud."

After the dance, we were given a charge to remember everything we'd learned in the program. A local minister came to pray for us. And then I was called up front to say a few words to my peers. I looked out among the crowd and saw my favorite hater. I knew Saxon and I were going to the same college. I had much to work out.

This time when I looked out in the crowd I saw someone I'd hurt. I realized I couldn't go back and change anything with me and Savoy. I knew I would pray for her and hoped she was healing. I took another deep breath and saw my family, who were all smiles. Seeing the peace in Damarius made me sigh one last time.

Then I opened with, "Being a gentleman is a tough responsibility and truly hard to achieve. It's harder to do the right thing than it is to do the wrong one. It takes a lot more energy to smile than to frown. I'm standing up here before you today, I think, by default. I don't feel like anyone's leader but I guess the Beau think otherwise. So I guess what I say to encourage them is what it takes to encourage me.

"Being an eighteen-year-old black male is a lot of pressure. It is so easy for us to fall into stereotypes of some of the men who have walked before us. Then when we feel pressured to be with the in-crowd, nobody wants to be called a punk. What's been motivating me lately has been inward pressure. Yeah I wanna please my parents, I wanna please myself, but deep down I wanna please God. And because He lives within me I can tap in on that pressure and walk right. I can't tell you what's going to be around the corner for any of us but I know the one who knows. And to my Beautillion brothers, falling in love with Jesus is the best thing I've ever done. He makes me feel better than any drop of alcohol I could drink. He makes me feel so high I think I can do anything, much better than a joint could make me feel.

"When I lose my girl to my own stupidity and I think I'm too big to be held in my mom's arms, I can stand out on the golf course and God can send a strong wind that engulfs me.

And then I feel loved by Him. We've gone through this program. We've all learned to be gentlemen and now let's continue to act like it. No one is leading us to do the wrong
thing. We're all leaders pressing hard for positive results and
coming out strong."

Perry Skky Jr., Book 2:

PRESSING HARD

Stephanie Perry Moore

ABOUT THIS GUIDE

The following questions are intended to
enhance your group's reading of
PRESSING HARD
by Stephanie Perry Moore

DISCUSSION QUESTIONS

1. Perry Skky Jr. doesn't want to be punked by his best buddy. Is his decision to prove he can hang a good choice or a bad one? How do you handle the pressure of standing up for what you know is right?

2. Because of Perry's choice to take a drink, he blacks out and finds himself in a compromised position. Do you think he learned anything from the party incident? If you made a bad choice once, how can you make sure you don't repeat your mistakes?

3. One of Perry's best friends reveals he owes a drug dealer, and Perry doesn't want to tell what he really thinks because he's being blackmailed by the same guy. Do you think Perry's stance to protect himself is the right one? What would you tell your friend in this situation?

4. Perry is confused when the head coach of the school of his choice is gone from the job. Do you think it's okay to rethink decisions you've made? What should you look for when you reevaluate your choices that you didn't think about the first time?

5. Damarius is sad that he isn't signing a letter of intent to go to college as are Perry and Cole. How does Perry address his friend's feelings? What are some ways you can support a friend when good things don't happen for them?

6. Perry catches his grandmother using a substance that is illegal. Though she claims it is for health reasons, do you feel Perry is correct in keeping this information to himself? How would you respond if an adult asks you to maintain a shady secret?

7. After the big basketball game a lot of the students get drunk. How does Perry try to help defuse the argument between Damarius and Ciara? What are ways you can help a friend not get into trouble?

8. Unfortunately, Ciara loses her life because of her drinking. Do you think anyone is to blame? What are the ways you can deal with the loss of a loved one?

9. Tori and Perry get very close after the funeral. Do you think they went too far for the wrong reasons? Where is the best place to go to find comfort to heal your hurting soul?

10. Perry feels pressure to break things off with Tori, and things blow up with him and Savoy. Do you think he'll learn how to combat pressures and temptations in other books in the series? How can you be moved by God to stay on the course He's planned for your life instead of being led down the wrong path?

Start Your Own Book Club

Courtesy of the PERRY SKKY JR. series

ABOUT THIS GUIDE

The following is intended to help you get
the Book Club you've always wanted
up and running!
Enjoy!

Start Your Own Book Club

A Book Club is not only a great way to make friends, but it is also a fun and safe environment for you to express your views and opinions on everything from fashion to teen pregnancy. A Teen Book Club can also become a forum or venue to air grievances and plan remedies for problems.

The People

To start, all you need is yourself and at least one other person. There's no criteria for who this person or persons should be other than a desire to read and a commitment to read and discuss during a certain time frame.

The Rules

People tend to disagree with each other, cut each other off when speaking, and take criticism personally. So, there should be some ground rules:

1. Do not attack people for their ideas or opinions.

2. When you disagree with a book club member on a point, disagree respectfully. This means that you do not denigrate another person for their ideas. There shouldn't be any name calling or saying, "That's stupid!" Instead, say, "I can respect your position, however, I feel differently."

3. Back up your opinions with concrete evidence, either from the book in question or life in general.

4. Allow every one a turn to comment.

5. Do not cut a member off when the person is speaking. Respectfully wait your turn.

6. Critique only the idea (and do so responsibly; again,

simply saying, "That's stupid!" is not allowed). Do not crit-
icize the person.

7. Every member must agree to and abide by the ground
   rules.

Feel free to add any other ground rules you think might be
necessary.

The Meeting Place

Once you've decided on members, and agreed to the ground
rules, you should decide on a place to meet. This could be
the local library, the school library, your favorite restaurant, a
bookstore, or a member's home. Remember, though, if you
decide to hold your sessions at a member's home, the location should rotate to another member's home for the next
session. It's also polite for guests to bring treats when attending a Book Club meeting at a member's home. If you choose
to hold your meetings in a public place, always remember
to ask the permission of the librarian or store manager. If you
decide to hold your meetings in a local bookstore, ask the
manager to post a flyer in the window announcing the Book
Club to attract more members if you so desire.

Timing is Everything

Teenagers of today are all much busier than teenagers of the
past. You're probably thinking, "Between chorus rehearsals,
the Drama Club, and oh yeah, my job, when will I ever have
time to read another book that doesn't feature Romeo and
Juliet!" Well, there's always time, if it's time well-planned and
time planned ahead. You and your Book Club can decide to
meet as often or as little as is appropriate for your bustling
schedules. *Once a month* is a favorite option. *Sleepover Book*

Club meetings—if you're open to excluding one gender—is also a favorite option. And in this day of high-tech, savvy teens, *Internet Discussion Groups* are also an appealing option. Just choose what's right for you!

Well, you've got the people, the ground rules, the place, and the time. All you need now is a book!

The Book

Choosing a book is the most fun. PRESSING HARD is of course an excellent choice, and since it's part of a series, you won't soon run out of books to read and discuss. Your Book Club can also have comparative discussions as you compare the first book, PRIME CHOICE, to the second, PRESSING HARD, and so on.

But depending upon your reading appetite, you may want to veer outside of the Perry Skky Jr. series. That's okay. There are plenty of options, many of which you will be able to find under the Dafina Books for Young Readers Program in the coming months.

But don't be afraid to mix it up. Nonfiction is just as good as fiction and a fun way to learn about from where we came without just using a history text book. Science fiction and fantasy can be fun, too!

And always research the author. You might find the author has a website where you can post your Book Club's questions or comments. You can correspond with Stephanie Perry Moore by visiting her website, www.stephanieperrymoore.com. She can sit in on your meetings, either in person, or on the phone, and this can be a fun way to discuss the book as well!

The Discussion

Every good Book Club discussion starts with questions. PRESSING HARD, as will every book in the Perry Skky Jr. series, comes along with a Reading Group Guide for your convenience, though of course, it's fine to make up your own. Here are some sample questions to get started:

1. What's this book all about anyway?

2. Who are the characters? Do we like them? Do they remind us of real people?

3. Was the story interesting? Were real issues of concern to you examined?

4. Were there details that didn't quite work for you or ring true?

5. Did the author create a believable environment—one that you could visualize?

6. Was the ending satisfying?

7. Would you read another book from this author?

Record Keeper

It's generally a good idea to have someone keep track of the books you read. Often libraries and schools will hold reading drives where you're rewarded for having read a certain number of books in a certain time period. Perhaps a pizza party awaits!

Get Your Teachers and Parents Involved

Teachers and parents love it when kids get together and read. So involve your teachers and parents. Your Book Club may read a particular book where it would help to have an adult's perspective as part of the discussion. Teachers may also be able to include what you're doing as a Book Club in the classroom curriculum. That way books you love to read such as PRESSING HARD can find a place in your classroom alongside the books you don't love to read as much.

Resources

To find some new favorite writers, check out the following resources. Happy reading!

Young Adult Library Services Association
http://www.ala.org/ala/yalsa/yalsa.htm

Carnegie Library of Pittsburgh
Hip-Hop!
Teen Rap Titles
http://www.carnegielibrary.org/teens/read/booklists/
teenrap.html

TeensPoint.org
What Teens Are Reading?
http://www.teenspoint.org/reading_matters/book_list.asp?
sort=5&list=274

Teenreads.com
http://www.teenreads.com/

Sacramento Public Library
Fantasy Reading for Kids
http://www.saclibrary.org/teens/fantasy.html

Book Divas
http://www.bookdivas.com/

Meg Cabot Book Club
http://www.megcabotbookclub.com/

Stay tuned for the next book in this series
PROBLEM SOLVED,
available November 2007 wherever books are sold.
Until then, satisfy your Perry Skky Jr. craving with
the following excerpt from the next installment.

ENJOY!

Now, I know better. When a white person looks at me, they either see a rising football star or just another hoodlum. I didn't get the latter look often because I was known for my moves on the field. I guess I was sheltered. I didn't have much interaction with people of a different culture or race. So when Saxon and I stood at the steel hotel doorway of our Beau party that was getting a bit out of control, and the manager stood in front of both of us looking like he wanted to grab us by the necks and throw us in jail, I didn't know how to take it. Racism was hitting me straight in the face. No part of me liked that.

But Saxon seemed to understand the man's attitude. He took the lead and said, "All right man, we hear you. We're just having a little fun. Dang. We pay our money just like everybody else. You just trying to get on us 'cause we're black."

"Now son, there's no need to toss the race card around," the red faced manager said, looking away.

"Wait, hold up," Saxon said as he leaned into the man's beaming red face. "I am not your son."

"Okay, you need to step back then," the manager asked, realizing he wasn't dealing with a punk.

Saxon and I had never been cool. Truthfully, we both had

egos. We were both *the man* at our perspective schools. It was going to be interesting playing ball with him at Georgia Tech in the next couple of months. He was a wild guy and I didn't have much respect for the dude. Yet, in some ways we were cut from the same piece of sirloin. And I felt a bond with him when the manager tried him.

Though there wasn't alcohol in the room where the party was jumping off, I wasn't a fool. I could smell Saxon had been tipping in someone's jar. The last thing he needed was to be hauled off for letting his mouth get the best of him. So I pushed him back into the room with the rest of the folks.

I said to the riled up guy, "I got this boy. Get in there."

Over my shoulder Saxon said, "Tell me something then. Because you'd better talk some sense into him. Shoot, I'm about to bust a—"

"Man, go," I said, grabbing the doorknob and trying to shut Saxon inside. "Sir, I'm sorry for my friend."

"You don't need to apologize for me," Saxon said as the door closed.

I looked over at the manager and said, "Really sir, we'll keep it down."

The manager nodded. "I'm just saying, young man, this is a respectable hotel. We didn't mind having your event in the ballroom, but we don't allow room parties. If you can assure me that you people will keep it down, then I won't bother you."

Again this man was ticking me off. *You people*, what in the heck did he mean by that? He backed away—I guess he saw fire in my eyes.

"Well, I'll leave you to your guests now," the manager said.

I closed the door in anger. Saxon came up to me, his breath was stronger than before.

"Want a little?" he said holding out a bottle of gin.

"Naw man, I'm straight," I said to him as I looked around the place for his gorgeous sister.

Saxon followed me. "See wh-white men think they can talk to the black man any kinda way. My dad gets that crap all the time on his job, but I won't ever let someone think they can handle me without dis...spect."

"You mean respect, Sax," I said, trying to keep up with what he was saying.

"Whatever, man, you know what I'm saying. You feel me too. I saw the heated look on your face when you came back in here. He said something that ticked you off, right?"

I didn't respond. Saxon grabbed my shirt. He shook me.

"Let's go jack him up. We need to teach him a lesson."

Taking his paws off me I said, "Boy, go party. We both need to cool down."

Then I looked for his sister. I couldn't get with her, though, because she was dancing with some other dude. But as I watched him rub his hands up her fine thighs I knew I had to let her know how I felt.

Before I could make my way over to her, I heard someone banging on the hotel door. My first thought was that the manager had come back too soon. And if it was him, maybe Saxon's idea wasn't such a crazy one after all.

Frustrated, I snatched the door open and said, "What?"

"Boy, you can't yell at that pretty lady," Saxon said over my shoulder at the sight of my sister. "Come in, come in."

"Sax, get back," I said as he tried to grab her butt. "Your cousin will get you, man, and my dad will too."

"Oh, Payton! Dang, that's Tad's girl? Payton, you look different," Saxon said. "I didn't mean no harm."

"We're cool, Sax," Payton said to him.

"What's up?" I asked her.

She said, "Mom and dad are in their room on the floor

below and want to see you. Folks have been complaining about the noise, Perry."

Dang, the music wasn't that loud.

"You staying or what?" I asked my sister.

"Naw, Tad is coming after he gets off and I gave him mom's room number."

Shutting the door as we entered the hall, I said sarcastically, "That was smart."

She hit me. Though Payton was kidding, I clammed up. We walked to the elevator in silence.

"What's up with you? I was just joking," she asked as she pushed the button for our parents' floor once we got on.

"Not you, sis," I said as we got off the elevator. "I'm just tired, that's all. And I don't want dad going off on me tonight. I'm not in the mood."

My dad opened the door as if he was waiting for me to arrive. "Junior, I can hear you guys."

I heard noise as well, but the bass beat sounded off. I figured I didn't need to argue with him. I'd let him speak his piece and then I'd be on my way.

"Look, you asked for your own room and I agreed to pay for it. Don't make me regret that decision. The hotel manager called me and said he's been getting complaints about the noise. I knew you were going to have some of your friends over, but boy, don't y'all tear up nothing. And kids can't be drinking in there. Be responsible."

"Dad, I got it," I let out before turning to head back.

"Junior, I'm not finished talking to you."

Sighing and facing him again, I said, "What else dad?"

"Look son, I'm not trying to spoil the party. If that was the case, I would have come down there myself. Just know the rules are different for black kids. Some white folks only tolerate so much. So don't give them a reason to shut down your fun, understand?" he asked.

"Got it."

He said, "Now Payton, go with him and make sure things stay in line."

"But dad, Tad's coming here," my sister said.

"Good, he and I need to have a little chat and then I'll send him your way. I don't want y'all too close." He shut the door on both of us.

My sister vented. "Ugh!"

She took the word right out my mouth. We looked at the elevator and saw a lot of people waiting for it. Payton suggested we take the stairs up one flight. I agreed. When we got around the corner, awfully loud rock music was coming from a room. I peered inside and saw tons of white kids jamming. Then it hit me. What my father was hearing was from around the corner not from above.

This blond-headed dude came out into the hall. "Hey, y'all are welcome to come in."

"Naw, man, we're straight," I said to him. "But tell me something—are you getting any complaints on the noise from the hotel?"

"Complaints? Naw dude," he looked at my sister with interest and smiled.

"That's my sister, but she's taken."

"Cool man, y'all come back," he said, swaying a little. He was just as drunk as Saxon.

Payton and I both laughed and headed to our jam. When we arrived, the hotel manager was walking back toward our door. I wanted him to ask me to keep things quiet.

"Mr. Skky, the noise seems to be growing from this room. I'm afraid I need you to ask your guests to leave. You understand?"

I laughed. "Sir, we just left the party down below us and they have their speakers blasting louder than ours. And since you're not asking them to curtail their fun, maybe you'd bet-

ter look the other way on our fun as well. Not unless you
want me to report this bias. Are you understanding me?"

"Oh well, Mr. Skky, no need to get upset. Just keep the
noise down as best you can. Sorry I bothered you," the manager turned and walked away.

I was glad I had caught him being unfair. But at least it felt
good fighting injustice the right way and winning.

Back in the room, the place seemed more packed than we
had left it and some of the people I saw in the small cramped
room hadn't even been at the ball.

I frantically scanned the room looking for Savoy and I
couldn't find her. I hoped she hadn't left. Even though I had
apologized before for messing up our relationship, somehow I felt I still needed to explain that I cared.

"Oh, so what's up? You looking for my cousin, huh?" Tad
said to me.

Tad and I were cool. I think he liked me a little bit better
than he liked his first cousin Saxon, Savoy's brother. And that
was probably because of my morals. I wasn't all the way on
the Holy Holy side of the scale, but I was certainly wasn't
slumming in the gutters with Satan like Saxon either. I had
done his cousin wrong and I didn't know how he felt about
that. I didn't even know if he knew what had gone down between the two of us.

"Oh, so what? You can't talk to me? I know you looking for
Savoy. And I know what went down between the two of
y'all." he said.

Tad surprised me by saying, "Man, look. I'm not perfect so
don't think that I am. I want to get with your sister so bad,
but you know I just ask the Lord to keep me wanting to
please him more than I want to please my own flesh. So far
that has helped. Everybody makes mistakes and my cousin

isn't perfect either. You guys are about to go to college, so there is no reason why y'all can't work something out."

"You think she'll listen?"

"I don't know. There she is over there," he said. "Why don't you go ask her?"

I nodded and headed over in her direction.

She wasn't smiling and she wasn't walking towards me. But she wasn't walking away, either.

"Hey!" I said when I got right up to her.

"Hey."

"Wanna dance?"

"I've been dancing all night. I'm a little tired of dancing," she said.

"You want to step outside in the hall and talk? We can walk around the hotel."

"Yeah, we can do that," she said.

I was so excited to have a bit of her time. I mean, I didn't deserve it. We said we were going to be in a committed relationship and I broke that vow less than a month after we made that commitment. How could she ever trust me again? But when I looked into her gorgeous dark brown eyes, I knew I had to try. It messed with me a bit to see her in someone else's arms. And although it was all my fault, if there was anything I could do to reverse it, I had to try.

"So what did you want to talk about?" she asked when we got outside by the pool.

Being a popular guy, I could tell when girls wanted to get with me. They would wink, laugh at nothing or stand real close to me; wear revealing clothes and sometimes even give me their underwear. But Savoy's distant stance was far from inviting. Her arms folded, she repeated, "What did you want to talk about?"

I didn't know how to begin so I looked away. Then she

replied, "You know what? Maybe this wasn't a good idea, the two of us being alone up under the moon, stars and all. I can't do this, Perry."

Before she walked away, I grabbed her hand. "I messed up. I told you I messed up. Wait Savoy, don't leave!"

"Why should I stay?" she asked

"Because you have to know how I feel."

She chuckled. "Come on, Perry. Your actions told me how you feel about me. I'm not angry with you. I told you that. But you can't expect me to forget that it happened."

"No, no. I know you can't forget, but I don't want you to dwell on it."

"Yeah, right!" she said, stepping away from me. "There are some nights I can't even sleep because all I can do is imagine you in Tori's arms."

"Okay, maybe we can't be boyfriend/girlfriend anymore. Maybe that was too strong of a title for us anyway, but can't we just hang out—do this thing, see where it takes us?"

"Why should I reinvest time in something that I tried and it didn't work out?"

I didn't hear what she was saying—all I could see was her juicy lips asking me to kiss them. So I did. At first she was resistant, pushing me back a little, but her lips never left mine. And then she melted some, and then I knew what I felt for her she felt for me as well. We weren't headed to the marriage altar or anything, but in that kiss, in that moment, in that embrace I knew we weren't through. And when we pulled away Savoy knew it too.

"I guess us spending time together in the end isn't going to hurt anybody, but I am ready to go back to the party now. Perry, I mean—we can't do this! Kissing me and all, why are you trying to confuse me? You cheated on me, okay?"

"I was wrong and stupid. I'm sorry! Can't you see I feel something for you?"

"Yeah and that's what worries me, because maybe what you're feeling is something that could get us both into trouble. I don't know, maybe it's not a good idea for the both of us to hang out. I gotta go back now."

She didn't even wait for me to catch up to her as she opened up the back door of the hotel and walked through the ballroom corridor. I wanted to reach out and pull her close to me, but I just had to realize that we weren't in that place in our relationship anymore and it was my fault. When the elevator door opened she had her hand on her hip and her mouth looked pissed.

When I moved to step in the elevator, she said, "You know what, I'm just going to take the stairs, I'll see you up there."

"I can walk with you," I said.

"Nah."

She let the elevator doors shut, with me inside. Alone. Or I thought I was alone; the white dude from the party was behind me, squatting in a corner on the floor.

"Dang, man, that must be your girl. She looks mad, dude, what did you do?"

Even though the beer had him talking sluggishly, his relationship senses were right on target.

"Man, you black boys are dumb. There's no way I'd let a girl with a butt looking that good get away from me." He went to press the elevator's buttons. "Open up the door I want to go talk to her."

"Aw naw partna, you stay back." I said as I grabbed his arm and took it off the buttons.

"That's where I know you! You're that state football dude that plays all good and going to Tech and all. I'm a Bulldog, man!"

"I hear yah partna."

"Well let me just say this, I always heard that black boys

have a lot of pride. And that might be fine but that's why you're in this here elevator with me instead of with that girl."

When the elevator opened again it was his floor. He said, "You better lay down your pride and think about what I'm saying and go after what you want, you understand?"

I never caught his name. He was cool and he was drunk, but he had a point. Savoy wasn't going to make it easy for me to get back in her good graces and maybe that made me like her even more.